A
NOBLE
CONTRACT

Matilda My

First published in 2024 by Matilda My
Copyright © 2024 by Matilda My
ISBN: 9798878982900

All rights reserved.
No part of this publication may be reproduced, stored in retrieval system, or transmitted in any form or by any means without the prior permission in writing of the publisher, nor be otherwise circulated in any form of binding or cover or other than that in which it is published and without a similar condition including this condition being imposed on the subsequent purchaser.

All characters and events in this publication are fictitious and any resemblance to real persons, living or dead, is purely coincidental.

Imprint
Matilda My
c/o autorenglück.de
Franz-Mehring-Str.15
01237 Dresden

To the girls who are drawn to the darkness, who find beauty in the broken and strength in the shadows, this book is for you.

May these words be a reminder that even in the embrace of villains, there is still light and love to be found.

Content Notes

This story contains explicit sexual content, profanity, violence, foul language, murder and topics that may be sensitive to some readers.

A NOBLE CONTRACT

ONE

At first glance, you wouldn't guess how many people he has killed. His dark truths are concealed behind a perfectly tailored suit and green eyes.

My mother says, he has never killed with his own hands.

My father says, he lets his men do the dirty work.

They both fear him. And they both want me to marry him.

The sound of a fork scratching porcelain pulls me out of my thoughts. My sister cuts the rest of the steak I left over. Too bloody.

"You're a lucky girl," she whispers in my ear.

My mother presses her perfectly painted lips together. She doesn't like it when we speak in hushed tones. It's not proper for a lady, she says.

"I'm cursed, and this is the worst day of my life," I whisper back.

The strings begin to play one of my favorite songs. I nervously tap my foot to the beat. I don't know if I've ever been more anxious than today.

The Marquis is dressed entirely in black. It is said that he wears a specific color for each day of the week. Today is Saturday.

"Believe me, if I were lucky enough to marry a man like him," Charlotte points in his direction as subtly as possible, but noticeable enough to make wrinkles appear on our mother's forehead, "I wouldn't make a face as if my period had just started."

"Charlotte, that's enough!" Our mother is a petite woman, but when she gets angry, even the strongest man would kneel before her. "Don't make me regret putting you on the guest list."

My knuckles turn white as I grip the napkin. My gaze drifts towards him. He knows I exist, but it wouldn't even cross his mind to look me in the eyes.

His cufflinks sparkle in the glow of the chandeliers. I wonder if he carries a weapon with him. And I wonder how his breath will sound at night when I lie by his side, whether he sleeps deeply or restlessly, like me. I wish I never had to find out these things.

"Do you think it can still be canceled?" My cold fingers find my sister's hand. She sighs.

"I don't think so, Louise. I guess it's decided."

Twenty-one years. For twenty-one years my family has made decisions for me. What sport I play, what school I attend, who my friends are. My nails dig into my sister's hand. I want to be free.

"Ouch, you're hurting me." She shakes her head and continues cutting the steak.

The Marquis has taken a seat at the table of honour, just a few meters away from us. I can't deny that he's a handsome man, but beauty cannot mask the scent of death.

A NOBLE CONTRACT

My father is wearing his best suit today. He gives me a proud smile. I am his life insurance. If he hadn't traveled to Italy two years ago, we wouldn't be in this situation today. But of course he takes no responsibility. I have to fight his battles for him, like I always have.

"You look beautiful," he says with a hoarse voice. "The Marquis will be mesmerized when he sees you."

I doubt it. He came with company. Sitting next to him is a woman so stunning that I internally pray that I will never be photographed next to her.

As if he sensed my gaze, he turns around. Our eyes meet. Cold sweat forms on the back of my neck. He pushes his chair back, rises to his full height, and apologizes with a slight bow to his companion. Then he approaches us.

His stride reveals that the world belongs to him. Or at least France. It is said that he resides in an apartment in the Palace of Versailles, but I don't believe it. He owns more than enough castles of his own.

I smell him before he stands in front of me. Lavender and masculinity and wealth. He extends his hand to my father, who jumps up from his chair so hastily that it almost topples backwards. My mother grabs the backrest at the very last moment.

My father wipes his hands on his tailored trousers before returning the Marquis' greeting. Something a gentleman like him would never normally do.

"Monsieur de Guise." Our family name sounds

wrong on the Marquis' tongue. Arrogant and cold, as if he's mocking our lineage.

"Monsieur de Colbert." My father's cheeks flush. I almost feel sorry for him. Almost...

I wish my father would speak with a prouder voice, but Albert has never been a courageous man, and for as long as I can remember, he's been kissing...

"Louise!" As if my mother has read my thoughts, her voice cuts through the air. "Where are your manners? Greet our *friend*."

I rise to my feet. My light green silk dress brushes against my knees. My lower lip trembles. Today marks the beginning of my end.

Girls like me are trained to function under pressure, under the merciless gaze of our world. Though I die a thousand deaths behind my cool facade, I manage the perfect curtsy. The Marquis bows. I am a circus animal, a trained monkey in designer shoes.

"It is an honor," he says. But it isn't. His smile mocks me. "You are truly as beautiful as they say." His vacant gaze doesn't see me. His words sound rehearsed. I don't respond.

With a single fluid motion, he takes hold of my hand. If he notices how cold it is, he doesn't show it. His lips brush my skin, then he straightens up and sizes up my dress. My mother chose it for me, and as his gaze glides along the fabric, I decide to burn it tonight, to erase the memory of him.

"So, the way things are going, we will see each

other at the Spring Ball?" He plays with his tie.

My mouth is too dry to respond. My mother jumps in for me.

"Louise feels delighted to accompany you. We are all looking forward to what the future will bring."

The future. Once a sweet promise, it now gives me nightmares. When I close my eyes and envision my future life, all I see are stuffy castle rooms, loneliness, and a husband who fills me with fear.

The Marquis bows before me once more. I can read in his gaze that he's disappointed by my appearance. But he knows as well as I do that our world consists of old rules, set by our ancestors, which we must unquestioningly follow. He must marry me, and I must submit to him.

"It was a pleasure, Louise. Until we meet again."

Albert extends his hand. Charlotte struggles to hold back a laugh. Sometimes, I hate my family.

On the way back home, I stare silently out of the window. The rest of the gala dinner passed calmly, uneventfully, without any further incidents.

My mother did what she does best - showering important people with the right compliments and boasting about Charlotte, my younger sister, who is still unmarried and therefore her main project now. Sometimes I wonder how our lives could have turned out if we had been born as ordinary girls.

I won't lie, it feels good to be wealthy. But my path has always been predetermined. The Marquis was an unfortunate coincidence. If I didn't have to marry him, another wealthy man would have entered my life instead. One thing I've known since birth is that I can't choose love.

Charlotte sits next to me in the backseat of the car. Our parents are driving separately from us. "I'm going to miss you so much," I say softly, and she gives me a tired smile.

"His estate is only two hours away," she runs her fingers through my hair. "We'll see each other more often than you think, even after you move in with him."

A lump in my throat makes it difficult to breathe.

"You know what I mean."

Her eyes fill with tears. We both know it. The Marquis will save my life, but my family will die.

TWO

My future husband is eleven years older than me. Today he turns 33 - and since his family doesn't celebrate birthdays, my mother forces me to visit him in person and give him a gift.

I mentally curse him for not having a party where I could stay in the background and anonymously place his gift on one of the designated tables. Now I'm forced to talk to him alone.

The driver turns into the driveway to his property. The wrought iron gate opens automatically. An avenue stretches in front of us, framed by trimmed bushes and fountains, which leads directly to the Marquis' castle.

Every detail of his gardens is perfectly staged. I expected nothing less. A servant opens the door for me, and I step out of the car.

The Marquis' castle is surrounded by many stories. It is said that one of his ancestors received it as a gift from Louis XIV and, as a token of gratitude, offered the king his youngest daughter as a mistress. She died only a few weeks later of poison, and supposedly her soul has never been able to detach itself from the old building. A shiver runs down my spine. This is where I will sleep, eat, dream.

Nervously, I cling to the box I brought, which contains the Marquis' gift.

A butler approaches me. "Mademoiselle de Guise. What an unexpected pleasure. Please follow me."

The fact that the staff already knows my name unsettles me. It makes my fate feel more definite.

I follow the older gentleman with timid steps. The Marquis' home is more than impressive. Our estate is large, but his is a kingdom. Countless corridors and halls lead me deeper into its dark heart. Gold and crystal pass me by. Old windows looking out into the garden.

Someone is playing the piano. The gentle melody grows louder as we cross the ballroom and the butler leads me up a narrow staircase that must have been intended for servants in earlier times.

As we come to a halt in front of an imposing door made of carved wood, I ask in a hushed voice, "Don't you want to know the reason for my visit? To announce me to the Marquis?"

The butler wrinkles his nose. "In this house, we do not ask questions," he replies, turning his back to me and opening the door.

The piano melody is so beautiful that it feels out of place in this cold setting. The gentle notes do not match the shadowy corners and endless corridors. I step through the door. The Marquis has his back turned to us. He sits at an old piano, playing.

Who would have thought that fingers that kill sounded like that?

The butler remains silently in the middle of the room so as not to interrupt his master. He waits patiently as the melancholic melody grows louder and quieter. I restlessly tuck a strand of hair behind my ear.

Finally, after what feels like an eternity, the music falls silent. The Marquis pauses, keeping his head lowered as if the notes still resonate within him.

"Rousel, you know that you must not disturb me at this hour," his voice dominates the room.

The butler runs a hand through his red hair.

"Forgive me, Marquis. But you requested that Mademoiselle de Guise be granted entry at any hour."

I am familiar with the traditions of the old wealthy world, and yet I feel uneasy.

At the sound of my name, the Marquis turns his head slightly. I can see his profile, the curve of his elegant nose, the strong chin.

"Leave us alone, Rousel," he says.

The man nods, turns on his heel, and closes the door behind him. We are alone. My future husband, whom I do not know, and I. He remains seated on the piano stool, his back turned to me.

"Louise," his broad shoulders move as he speaks. Today, he's wearing a dark red suit. "What brings me the honor of your visit?"

I notice that he doesn't use my title, a subtle hint that he considers himself superior to me. In rank, in wealth, in power. The gift box in my hands suddenly feels too heavy.

"I have come to congratulate you on your birthday. I... have brought a gift."

He slowly straightens up. As he turns towards me, he adjusts his suit and fixes his dark blonde hair. Even though there are several meters between us, I can feel him close to me, his overpowering presence.

His cynical smile sends a chill through me. "That's not necessary, Louise. For me, it's just another day." He takes a slow step towards me. "Birthdays are meant to torment us, to remind us that we will die, whether we want to or not."

My palms start to sweat. He stops in front of me, and I don't know what to do with my gift as he doesn't reach for it.

"It's rude to refuse a gift," I say softly. I want to appear confident in front of him, knowing that he will tear me apart the moment I show weakness, but I've heard too many dark stories about him to swallow my fear.

He tilts his head, his gaze piercing into mine. "Is that so?"

We stand in silence for a few seconds, facing each other. Eventually, he takes the box from my hands, unties the ribbon, and looks inside.

My father has chosen the gift for him.

It's a fountain pen that once belonged to Marie Antoinette's brother-in-law. With a skilled grip, the Marquis removes it from its holder and examines it against the light.

"Pretty."

Only a man like him could receive such a gift with such detached coolness. He looks down at me, his cheeks perfectly shaved.

"Did you choose this for me, Louise?". A slight smile plays on his lips.

"My father did." Blood rushes to my cheeks, I can feel myself blushing. "To be honest, I don't know you well enough to have an idea of what you might like. Albert has a better instinct for such things than I do..."

His thin smile mocks me.

"What I might like..." he says softly, barely audible. The words fade away amidst the thick carpets and heavy oil paintings. The piano room smells of old books and wood.

The Marquis places the fountain pen back into its box and sets it on one of the golden coffee tables.

"Thank you, Louise. I appreciate it. Your father has always been a man with excellent taste," he says, invitingly gesturing towards the chaise lounge, which is situated in an alcove at the other end of the room. I follow his hand and sit down. He himself takes a seat opposite me on one of the silk-covered stools.

The problem with men like him is that you can never know when they're lying. Beautiful words come naturally to them.

Maintaining composure means showing respect to his own family name, and that's why his smile can mean anything.

He hates me.

He likes me.

I'm insignificant to him.

He leans forward and reaches for a porcelain teapot. The aroma of warm tea has a calming effect on me.

"Please". His long fingers gesture towards one of the cups. I reach for it, clutching onto it as if the painted swans on the porcelain could free me from my life, carrying me away to another world.

The Marquis isn't even close to my type. His face is beautiful in a classical way, reminiscent of old paintings and statues in my grandfather's collection. I know that most women would kill to be in my position. At 33 years old, the Marquis is the most sought-after bachelor on the market. Wealthy, educated, eloquent.

But I am missing the honest gaze. I can only fall in love with eyes that reveal the soul behind them, and there are too many lies written in the Marquis's green.

He looks out of the window. On a meadow beneath the castle, black horses gallop in circles. A man stands in their midst, shouting.

"What truly brings you here?". The Marquis drops a pink sugar cube into his tea, stirs it with a golden spoon, and then slides it between his lips. He looks at me inquisitively.

"I wish I could be the spoon," Charlotte would say now.

"It's your birthday. No one should be alone on their birthday."

He shakes his head. "Let loneliness be my concern, Louise. Let's lay our cards on the table. Your parents sent you to me so that we can get to know each other better, didn't they?"

My flushed cheeks betray that he is right.

"We are going to get married - and we haven't spent a single moment together. Alone. That's why you're here. To get used to me... Because even though your parents are selling you off like a stallion, they still love you and want you to be prepared for me."

His words cut through my heart. The way he speaks to me is the closest thing to an insult from him.

Now I have my answer.

He hates me.

I know that he loves someone else.

"Maybe."

He leans forward, his gaze dissecting me. He delves into my memories, searching for my weaknesses.

"Let's be completely honest with each other. You do like honesty, don't you?"

I can't help but notice that his tone sounds as if he's speaking to a toddler. My head nods on its own accord.

"Our marriage won't be what you dreamed of as a young girl." As his penetrating gaze remains fixed on me, not giving me an inch of breathing space, I look out the window and try to focus on the black horses.

"I am not the prince you were promised when you were a child. I won't fulfill any of your dreams - and especially, you won't discover a warm side of me that reveals itself over time. To... endure our marriage," he clears his throat, "you will have to accept from the beginning that I cannot love you. There is no hope for us to grow closer or get to know each other better. Our marriage is purely a formality. Do you understand?"

My face burns with shame. I fold my hands in my lap and nod silently.

"Bravo." He continues to stir his spoon in the cup, the scraping of gold against porcelain driving me crazy.

"Do you know the reason why your parents asked me to marry you?"

I know it and I don't. I know half-truths, fragments, vague answers from my father, and whispers behind closed doors that I press my ear against.

"Our families have been connected for a long time. Our grandfathers were friends..."

"Friends," he stifles a laugh. It is not proper to interrupt a lady in the middle of a sentence, and the fact that he does so reveals that he's in no way trying to impress me. "They belonged to the same circle. They were more than friends."

"Okay, whatever." My patience is slowly wearing thin. The Marquis seems to notice. With an arrogant gesture of his hand, he signals for me to continue speaking.

"My father has... problems. And your family still owes mine a favor. After what my grandfather did for yours."

The shadows on his face grow darker, but if my words unsettle him, he doesn't show it. I tell him nothing he doesn't already know.

"Exactly. Problems." He sets his cup aside. "Which translates to your father trying to deceive the wrong people and paying for it with his life. And that of his family."

My throat burns. Don't cry, Louise, don't cry. Not in front of him.

"Albert knows that no one touches what belongs to me. I will save your life by marrying you, just as your grandfather once saved one of our lives. A life for a life. That settles our debt."

Honor is the foundation of our world. A favor holds more significance than mere altruism. It is politics. In our circles, showing weakness can lead to your downfall, and asking someone for help is akin to admitting defeat.

A favor does not expire and obligates until eternity. Until the debt is repaid. The Marquis is indebted to our family. That's why he hates me. That's why my life will be bleak and cold, but at least I will be alive while my mother, father, and sister lie beneath damp earth.

If my mother fails to marry Charlotte before my father's… old acquaintance strikes, I will lose the most important person in my life.

The Marquis has no siblings. He could never empathize with what I feel.

There is nothing written in his gaze except indifference and pride.

"I know you're afraid of me. That's good. This fear will prevent you from making reckless mistakes. I also know that you don't want to marry me. Believe me, I share your feelings. This union is everything I never hoped for in life. But the rules of our world cannot be changed - and we are just chess pieces destined to follow the moves of our ancestors. Accept it before your little heart breaks."

THREE

"How big is his… you know what?"

The only good thing about moving out soon will be that I'll have my own realm, without a sister who doesn't respect my privacy, paints her toenails on my freshly made bed, and asks intrusive questions.

"How should I know? We had tea, nothing more."

A red dress lands on the left pile, a light blue one on the right. I'm sorting out what I won't need in my new life.

"You're telling me you didn't sneak a look at his crotch? Louise! You have to know what to expect."

Yellow dress to the left.

I know that the Marquis will buy me an entirely new wardrobe once I live with him. However, I can't bring myself to part with my favorite dresses. They will be one of the few connections to my old life.

I raise an eyebrow at my sister's words.

"You do realize that our marriage will be purely formal, right? The last thing we're going to do is having sex."

She giggles and falls backwards onto my bed.

"Be careful with that nail polish! You know how much I hate it when you make a mess on my bed," I scold her, reaching out to steady the bottle before it spills.

"The Marquis is a man who lives for traditions. Of

course, he will insist on spending the wedding night with you and... consummating the marriage," she says, imitating our mother's voice in a high-pitched and shrill manner. That does make me laugh.

"Will you pray for me that he doesn't insist on it?" I say, feeling sick at the thought. The Marquis is tall and intimidating, definitely not made for a girl like me.

I am a virgin, and as I am facing a loveless marriage, it should remain that way for the rest of my life.

"The way he moves, he must be great in bed." Charlotte stares at the ceiling with a glassy gaze and I try not to think about the images flashing through her mind.

I grab a pillow and hit her in the face with it. "Pull yourself together. That's just disgusting."

"Hey!" she protests, snatching the pillow away from me. "Don't act like what I'm saying isn't true."

When I don't respond, she sticks her tongue out at me. "You will find out soon enough anyway - and be able to tell me if I'm right."

With a sad sigh, I sit down on the edge of the bed. "I'm scared, Charlotte."

She straightens up, being my only solace in this world. "I know. Me too."

I can't bring myself to look at her as I say, "Do you think Mother will find a husband for you in time... someone who will protect you?"

The truth is a hungry beast, feeding on dead hope

and wasted love.

"I hope so," she whispers. "But even if not, you are safe. That's what matters most."

I force myself to look into her eyes.

"It's not fair. Why did they sell *me* to the Marquis? Why do I get a chance to live while you might..." I can't bring myself to say it.

Charlotte smiles wearily and places a comforting hand on my shoulder.

"Because you're the eldest daughter. You know how it works. First come the firstborns, and then... the rest."

I gaze at us in the mirror. Despite what most people would claim, we don't look alike. At first glance, we have the same dark hair, the same bright eyes, but upon closer inspection, one can see Charlotte's wild features and my reserved ones, her courage and my... ordinariness.

She's always been better than me at everything. Riding, dancing, school - and I always cheered her on. Because I love her. Because it's easier for me to fade into the background anyway.

I can't believe my parents didn't choose her to marry the Marquis. I don't deserve to be saved, not if it means my sister has to die.

"Don't worry about me," she hugs me from the side. "I'll find a way to survive. I always have."

During dinner, Mother asks the question of all questions.

"Did the Marquis like your gift?"

My gift - chosen and paid for by my father. Albert puts on an innocent face. I look up from my plate. "Hard to say. The man is colder than the ice in Antarctica."

Beside me, my sister bursts into laughter. She loves it when I challenge Mother.

"Pull yourself together, Charlotte," Mother says, a furrow of anger crossing her face as she takes a calming sip of her wine.

"What did he say?"

"Pretty," I imitate the Marquis with a deep robotic voice.

"He has never been one for grand words," Albert hastily interjects before Mother suffers a stroke. "He shows his gratitude through actions."

"By the way," Mother wipes her mouth with her napkin. "We will be going to our tailor tomorrow so he can take your new measurements. Your bust has grown quite a bit lately. The atelier has been waiting for days to finally start working." Suspicion rises within me. "Measurements for what?"

"Your wedding dress."

My stomach twists. Wedding dress. I don't want it. "Doesn't that have time?"

"The wedding is less than three months away. We are already extremely late. The guest list is still not finished, and…"

"No." The determined tone of my voice surprises even myself. "I am not ready yet."

Mother sets aside her napkin. Charlotte and Albert hold their breaths.

"And I am not willing to have this conversation with you, my child."

"I am not a child anymore. I am 21."

"Exactly. Too young to die."

A pang shoots through my heart. My mother never calls a spade a spade. She never openly acknowledges hurdles to overcome, always pretending that everything is fine. The fact that she speaks so bluntly about the danger looming over us leaves me speechless.

This is not how I know her. Her eyes darken. "You have no idea what is at stake. How much effort and persuasion it took to convince the Marquis of our plan. You can't just throw it all away."

I am afraid of her.

"Do you know that he was already in a relationship before we made our agreement?"

I nod.

"And that he had to break off that connection to settle his debt with our family?"

My lower lip starts bleeding from how hard I'm biting on it.

"He left the woman he truly loves - for you. To protect you."

"Or maybe to fulfill the favor he still owes you?" I love my sister for her honesty. She puts things on the table, even if it's uncomfortable. Mother grows even paler, all the blood draining from her face.

"Be that as it may, what's important is that he will provide you with the security you need. Keep behaving so childishly, and he might reconsider."

Albert interrupts her. "I don't think so, darling. The Marquis is a man who doesn't break his word."

His gaze shifts to me. I rarely see him this serious. "You will marry him, Louise, whether you want to or not. Or I will end your life with my own hands."

FOUR

Before my father ruined us, I wanted to study. For as long as I can remember, I've lost myself in books, and at the age of seven, I decided to study literature one day. I wanted to get lost in libraries for days on end and wander between the pages of myths and legends.

Before my father ruined us, I picked a university in Paris, dreaming of a life far from obligations and full of friends who didn't know my family name. I wanted to hide our wealth and just be who I am: Louise with too big dreams, who starts stuttering when she has to speak in front of people.

Instead, I find myself sitting in the backseat of a Bentley, being driven to Monsieur Peyrot, our tailor. He has accompanied all the important moments of my life - from my baptism, to my first day of school, to my communion - and adorned them with breathtaking dresses. I know that he will work his magic once again this time.

His studio is packed with boxes of old buttons, thread, and lace. In front of the dark green walls, open shelves are filled with bolts of fabric in every color imaginable.

He greets me with a bow, and I marvel at how happy I am to see him. Every person who doesn't share our family secrets helps my soul breathe more freely.

Monsieur Peyrot isn't himself without a red pincushion around his wrist and his measuring tape around his neck. With great concentration, he takes my measurements.

My mother looks restless, glancing at her phone. I don't want to know what's bothering her.

"Can I choose any fabric I like?" I ask innocently instead.

"No," she curtly rebukes me. "The Marquis has clear ideas about how you should look on your big day."

The Marquis, the Marquis, the Marquis. I can't stand hearing his name anymore. I wish Charlotte were here, with one of her cheeky comments to lighten the mood, but Mother forbade her from coming along. Instead, she has to accompany Albert to a horse race. Maybe I *did* get the better end of the deal after all.

"To be honest, I don't care about his expectations. It's my wedding too, not just his, and the Marquis can kiss my ass."

"Let's save that for after the wedding."

I hold my breath. *Merde!*

He stands in the doorway, majestic and refined, living up to his powerful ancestors. His dark blond hair falls in perfect waves over his forehead. He looks younger than 33, thanks to his large green eyes.

"Monsieur de Colbert, I apologize profusely, she didn't mean it that way…" Mother tries to save the situation with an anxious voice, but he dismisses her with a bored wave of his hand.

"Let's not talk about it."

I hate his arrogant demeanor. Monsieur Peyrot does his best not to look like he's eavesdropping as he measures my waist.

Challengingly, I glare at my fiancé.

"To be honest, I *did* mean it that way. Minus the part where you kiss my ass."

He smirks. I can't believe it. Mother is too shocked to speak.

"Such a shame," he replies curtly. My face turns beet red.

He starts pacing around the room.

"Did you attend a school for proper etiquette, Louise?" What a question. "Otherwise, I can arrange tutoring for you. It's important to me that my future wife knows how to behave."

I clench my fists. "It's *my* wedding and *my* dress. I won't let myself be dressed up like a mindless doll. I have a say in what I wear."

He slowly runs his thumb over his lips. "Very well, as long as it's not excessive."

I take a deep breath. That's the best I can get out of him.

Mother has regained her composure by now. She strides gracefully towards him, her shoulders pushed back. She loves to criticize my poor posture and used to make me walk through the halls of our castle with books on my head as a child.

"What brings us the honor of your visit, Monsieur de Colbert? Honestly, I wasn't expecting you today."

He doesn't even look her in the eyes, instead, he watches intently as Monsieur Peyrot works on me.

"A business partner had to cancel our meeting last minute, so I unexpectedly had some free time."

If my mother is good at one thing, it's kissing asses in a rather shameless way.

"Is it about the deal with the Veenendaal family?"

He shakes his head, still not looking away from me. "No. Van den Berg. The negotiations are dragging on."

He steps closer to me. I have to tilt my head back to look into his eyes. He's so tall. With all my strength, I force my face to show no emotion. Only those who are cold and indifferent can survive in our world. His Adam's apple moves up and down.

"Spare no expense or effort, Peyrot," he speaks, looking at me. "I want the sight of my bride to silence all the doubters who gossip about our union. I want her to be the most beautiful woman France has ever seen."

He bows before me, then before my mother, and heads towards the door. "After Marie Antoinette, of course," he winks, referring to the fountain pen I've given him.

My heart almost leaps out of my chest, and even as I hear the sound of his car's engine fading in the distance, it takes all my strength not to show how helpless I feel.

FIVE

I will only be allowed to move into my new home after the wedding, but Mother managed to convince the Marquis to show me the chambers that will be ours beforehand.

Despite her strictness, she does her best to alleviate some of my fears. She herself was married to my father when she was sixteen, and although they became friends over the years, they never truly loved each other. She had already given her heart away to a stable boy of her father's. She never saw him again after the wedding.

It could be worse, I think as I ascend the stone stairs to the Marquis' castle. *At least I'm not in love with someone else whom I have to leave behind for this marriage.*

I have never been kissed. Never been touched by a man. Perhaps it's karma. Born into wealth, but never feeling love. Fate is a balance.

Rousel, the butler, leads me inside the castle as he did last time. A part of me hopes to catch a glimpse of the Marquis. Any detail I can gather about him before it gets serious is important. Every encounter, every brief conversation helps me better understand what awaits me.

My expectations are quickly shattered when Rousel himself begins to guide me through my future chambers.

"Is the Marquis not at home?" I ask as I step through a set of double doors behind him. Rousel wrinkles his nose. I know I am being too curious. "He is currently out of the country."

I want to ask further, but instead, I bite my tongue. I don't care where he is.

My bedroom is beautiful, adorned in a delicate pale yellow, filled with antique furniture covered in precious silk. The bed can be closed off with thick curtains, and the floor-to-ceiling windows offer a perfect view of the gardens.

It's a dream, but a lonely one. It lacks visitors, voices, a barking dog or a purring cat. The beauty that surrounds me is so desolate that I can hardly believe someone truly lives here.

"How many weeks of the year does the Marquis spend at home?"

Rousel runs his finger along an old dresser and grimaces disapprovingly as dust clings to it.

"Eight to twelve."

"Months?"

"Weeks."

Of course. "So, I will be living here alone?"

"The staff is always around."

A man like Rousel is incapable of understanding that a twenty-one-year-old woman needs more company than just a butler and the maids.

Yes, I am ungrateful. But in the past, I have often tried to befriend the staff, and they have always avoided me because their position forbids them from speaking openly with me. Yet, I have always preferred spending time with them over the haughty personalities of my own circles.

I know that my marriage will save my life. But the thought of spending the rest of it alone in this castle, with a man who neither touches nor appreciates me, feels like being buried alive.

Alongside my bedroom, I will own a parlor, a dressing room, and a bathroom almost entirely made of marble. I must not complain. I am privileged. Yet, my heart knots in my chest.

Rousel finishes his tour, and I smile at him with innocent eyes. "Is it alright if I stay a little longer? I need some time to get used to the idea of living here."

This time, I am grateful for his blind loyalty and his tendency not to ask questions. He simply nods and bids me farewell with a brief bow. "Let me know when you are ready. I will escort you to the exit."

Like hell I will. I wait only for the sound of his footsteps to fade away. Once I'm certain that I'm rid of him and his keen eagle eyes, I begin to spy. I want to know where the Marquis sleeps - whether we will be living close to each other and if there are any doors connecting his rooms to mine that I need to barricade.

I am curious. I want to learn more about the man around whom all the dark stories revolve, who hovers like a shadow over everything because he's more powerful than any other head of the other families.

I want to know what makes him so influential and what he's hiding.

Through a hidden door in my bedroom, I enter a staircase. The plain steps lead me up another floor. As I open a door, I know that I'm in the right place. I've found the room where he met me last time.

Since I doubt that his staff enters his chambers in his absence, I confidently move to the center of the room. No one will disturb me.

"Good evening."

A velvety voice interrupts my trance. It belongs to a woman...

"Can I help you?"

I immediately recognize her. A woman like her is unforgettable. Her beauty is unique. She was his companion the evening we met for the first time.

"I... I'm sorry," I begin to stutter. "I didn't know anyone was here. I... I got lost."

She rises from the chair where the Marquis sat during my last visit. She is tall, graceful, and slender. Her light blonde hair cascades like a rain of gold over her slim shoulders. With unique elegance, she approaches me.

"Happens to the best of us. In a castle like this, one must be careful not to take the wrong path," she says, winking at me.

She reminds me of a modern-day Lucrezia Borgia. So beautiful that one longs to die at the sight of her.

It's hard to guess her age, but her confident stride and way of speaking tell me that she must be older than me. She extends a hand towards me.

"Madison. Nice to meet you."

Only now do I notice her American accent. It's impressive how well she hides it behind her perfect French.

"Louise," I reply.

"I've heard about you." Her warm smile makes her even more beautiful. "You are Jeromes' fiancée."

The sound of his name on her tongue catches my attention. She notices my questioning expression and speaks before I can ask any questions.

"I am the woman he left for you."

SIX

The Marquis

I can see the fear in their eyes. Every. Damn. Day.

Whatever I do, the people around me are afraid. When I give my driver the address to where he should take me. When I play the final round of cards with friends. When I instruct the stable master to ride the horses hard.

Every word makes them freeze and listen to the sound of my voice, trying to figure out if I'm having a good day or if I'm on the verge of slitting someone's throat.

The world must fear you, only then can it be yours, my father used to say to me, and he was right. He feared me seconds before I put a bullet through his head.

I always knew that my role could only be carried by a man who loves solitude. I am made for solitude.

Right now, it's too loud. With the palm of my left hand, I strike the table once. The powerful men of the world around me freeze. They stare at me.

"Good morning, gentlemen." My voice sounds tired. I landed in New York before sunrise and will already be flying back in the evening.

I know no fear, but at the thought of the last item on the agenda, I inwardly roll my eyes. Talking about it seems like a pure waste of time.

Louise's father sits to my right. I despise him, and

I despise the fact that he gets to occupy the seat next to me now that we are related.

The group keeps discussing which Ivy League college should be honored with a new fund. It has never been as difficult for me as it is today to stay focused.

As the sun sets, we come to the final point.

"Gentlemen, as you may have heard, we have a new union to celebrate." I almost let myself drum my fingers on the table.

Being the chairman of this circle is not easy. All eyes are always on me. "As you know, I am not a man of many words. Let's keep it brief. In less than three months, I will be marrying Louise de Guise. Save the congratulations."

A wave of mixed emotions floods the room. I can see Albert's wide grin from the corner of my eye and make a mental note to break his nose before Gino murders him.

Gino. The eldest member of our group. He sits across from me at the other end of the table. I know he is just waiting for an opportunity to dethrone me. But I am not his primary target at the moment. It's Albert.

I dismiss the group. Twelve men in tailored suits rise from their chairs, shake hands with each other, and prepare to fly back to their respective home countries. Tokyo. Chicago. London.

There are politicians who show their faces openly and pretend to be powerful, and then there's us, the ones who actually hold the strings and determine the fate of the world.

We operate in secrecy. In private jets, ballrooms, and secluded conference rooms on the 51st floor.

I'm about to close the door when I notice a shadow behind me. Someone has stayed behind. Slowly, I turn around.

Gino stands before me. He's not tall, but his presence can fill any room and conquer any opponent.

He speaks with a thick Italian accent. "Congratulations on your engagement, my son."

The irony in his voice is almost painful. He feels betrayed by me. He's done business with my grandfather and we've always been close confidants. The fact that I'm now marrying the daughter of the man who tried to cheat him out of his fortune is something he finds hard to forgive me for.

"I had no choice," I reply calmly. "You know that."

Gino nods. "I understand, my son." He places a hand on my shoulder. "And hopefully, you understand that I will still kill him."

I can't help but grin. "Do as you please. It suits me just fine. His grandfather saved mine's life. The debt of my family is settled through this marriage. The rest doesn't matter to me."

Gino smells of sweat and cigars. I admire and despise him in equal measure.

"That's not enough for me." His serious gaze pierces into my soul. "I don't like being taken for a fool."

I shift my weight from one leg to another. I fear no one, but Gino is the most unpleasant of all potential adversaries because he possesses endurance and never forgets.

"I don't like that this son of a bitch managed to save his daughter. He knows I won't lay a finger on her once she's your wife. Because we… are friends. He outsmarted me."

Though he maintains composure, I can sense that the gates of hell have been opened within Gino.

"I won't harm a hair on her head. Unless…" I don't like the look in his eyes. "Unless you give me permission to do"

Not returning a favor is one thing, but breaking a promise is akin to committing a mortal sin.

"You want me to lose my honor by not keeping my word and allowing you to harm her?"

Gino curls his lips. It's evident that he's thought long and hard about the words he will choose to convince me.

"My son, you *are* keeping your word. You *are* marrying her. That's all you promised."

Thoughtfully, I gaze out of the window at the lights of New York City. From up here, the rest of the world seems insignificant. Louise doesn't matter to me. She is young and beautiful. Nothing more. There is no connection between us.

Still, I hesitate. I can't explain why.

Pull yourself together. Remember who you are. Who

you want to be.

"Agreed," I say, gripping his hand firmly as we lock eyes. "Let a year pass after the wedding, so that no one suspects anything. After that, you may kill her."

SEVEN

Madison scares me. She is polite and gives me no reason to dislike her, but she embodies everything I will never be. Independence. Strength. Perfection.

We've been sitting across from each other in the Marquis' piano room for about half an hour, talking about everything under the sun.

She wants to get to know me better. I can't fathom why. She should hate me. I am the reason she cannot marry the man she loves. Instead, we drink tea and laugh at the most absurd things.

"You're funny," she blurts out with tears in her eyes. "I'm starting to almost like you."

Almost.

"How old are you, Louise?"

"21."

Her friendly expression turns into mockery. "I didn't realize Jerome had a thing for children."

The atmosphere in the room turns icy in an instant. Her beautiful face loses its warm mask and suddenly appears hardened. Bitter.

It's strange to hear the Marquis' first name spoken aloud. No one ever calls him by his real name. Jerome…

"Do you know the story of how we met?" She relaxes back into her chair, not waiting for my response before continuing.

"He saw me from behind at his friend's birthday party, and even before he looked at my face, he had fallen in love with me. Because he felt the connection between us, an invisible string that already bound us back then… and will always bind us."

I don't know why she's telling me this.

"Are you here to inspect your future chambers?"

"Yes."

She twirls a blonde lock of hair around her finger and gazes thoughtfully outside.

"Yellow is my favorite color," she says, more to herself than to me. "He had the rooms designed for me. I was supposed to live there."

I feel sorry for her. While I can't fully understand her pain, I know how difficult it is to let go of someone you love.

Still, her cold tone suffocates me. I want to escape this encounter.

"I hadn't planned on… marrying him."

She looks at me, and for the first time, I feel like she truly sees me, examining me and searching for flaws that would prove I will forever be a cheap substitute.

"Maybe not you. But your parents certainly did." Her voice grows softer as she leans forward. "They took what should have been mine."

A car pulls up in the courtyard.

"You will fall in love again. I'm sure of it." I can't think of anything better to say.

She smiles cynically and shakes her head almost

imperceptibly. "Oh no, my dear. You would like that, wouldn't you? For me to hand over my man to you and give up without a fight."

"That's not what I meant."

"It's alright. You're just a child. You don't yet understand the situation you've gotten yourself into."

She slowly stands up and walks towards the piano, where the Marquis played during my last visit. Absentmindedly, she runs her fingers along the surface of the keys.

"You are heading towards a loveless marriage. Jerome has already given his heart away, and men like him only do that once in their lives. He may have promised your father to take you in, but that doesn't mean he will be willing to give me up."

She is convinced that I want to compete with her. Fight for the Marquis' heart. This misconception couldn't be further from the truth - and yet, her words hurt. Because despite my dislike for my fiancé, despite all the resistance I put up against this new life, it still hurts how unlikely she sees the possibility of him falling in love with someone like me.

"We will live here together," she turns around and looks into my eyes. "You will mean nothing to him. Not even be his little toy. He will pass you in the mornings without even acknowledging your presence when you wish him a good day. You will have dinner together, and as you tell him about the insignificant events of your day, he will only be thinking about how he fucks me at night. Every single second, you will regret robbing me of the life that should have been mine."

That's too much. I'm not usually one to get emotional, but her truths pierce my heart like poisonous arrows. Because it's true. Because she will be proven right, and I will wither away in this castle like a forgotten flower.

Gasping for air, I jump up. I need to get out of here. Madison's triumphant smile burns into my teary eyes. Without another word, I storm towards the door.

It opens on its own, just seconds before I reach it. Someone enters. It's the Marquis, dressed in a black suit. Exhaustion is written all over his face. When he spots us, his mouth drops open in astonishment. He wants to say something, but I beat him to it.

"You can forget about the wedding. I will never set foot in this house again, and I would rather die than become your wife," my voice is shrill, my breath too fast.

I push past him, out into the hallway. I want to run, but he grabs my wrist. His grip is strong. He could break my bones.

"Let go of me right now!" Tears stream down my face.

His eyes sparkle, his mouth tightens. "What is going on here?" he hisses, looking at me and then at Madison with a questioning gaze.

"Nothing," she purrs. "We're just getting to know each other. One can never have too many friends."

He's distracted, and that's my chance. I open my mouth and sink my teeth into his hand with all my strength. He jerks back. I am free and I run, run, run until my lungs burn more painfully than my heart.

The butler waits at the entrance of the house.

"Rousel!"

He flinches.

"Call me a car. I want to go home."

EIGHT

Three days pass without hearing from him. On the fourth day, the Marquis sends a card. It's served to my mother on a golden tray during dinner. Just one sentence, written in ink.

Does your daughter really value her life so little?

After my escape from the Marquis, I had hoped he would release me. But as his message arrives, I realize that he would never cancel the wedding, no matter how deeply I insult him.

He has announced to the Circle that I will be his wife. Dissolving the union now would be his downfall.

A man like him, who rules the dark depths of our world, must appear steadfast and cannot deviate from decisions made.

After dinner, I take a walk in our gardens with Charlotte. They are smaller than the Marquis', but nowhere near as dreary. My family loves flowers and cherry trees.

"How do you feel?" Her voice sounds gentle.

Since I told her about my encounter with Madison, she handles me with kid gloves. I had to convince her with all my might not to personally go to the

Marquis' castle and tear his girlfriend's head off.

"I'm fine, Charlotte, really."

Her life is at stake and she's worried about me. My beloved compassionate sister.

"Honestly, I don't know what to think of him anymore," she says. "I mean, I found him sexy and all, but the whole two women thing makes him really unattractive."

"He only has one woman. Madison. I will be his bride on paper, but I can't change his heart - and I don't want to."

Charlotte puts an arm around my shoulders as we make our way to our favorite spot, the pond under the weeping willow.

"There's surely a handsome stable boy working for him, who can distract you."

I roll my eyes. "As if I'm allowed to fall in love with someone else."

"But it's okay for him to do so?"

The old tree, on whose branches we spent entire days as children, whispers in the wind.

"You know very well that different rules apply to us women. He is the Marquis. He can take as many lovers as he wants. I, on the other hand, must nod, smile politely, and preferably make myself invisible in public. I need him to survive, and he only needs me for official events, to parade me on his arm."

Charlotte plucks a flower and tucks it behind my ear. "You should stop underestimating yourself." Her blue eyes sparkle. "Don't forget what you can gain from him."

"I don't want his money."

"That's not what I'm talking about."

The wind carries the flower away. "You can ask him to help me. My only chance of survival is to marry an influential man who can protect me from Gino. Father has lost the respect of our friends. But the Marquis… his friends are powerful. If you can persuade him to set me up with one of them, it could save my life."

We don't know how or when Gino will strike. It could be three years or three days from now. He could swiftly and painlessly shoot my family or torture them in a cellar for months. All we know is this: my father made a mistake – and Charlotte is right: the Marquis is our last chance to undo it.

NINE
The Marquis

Odin van den Berg is the most draining business partner I have ever dealt with. I have broken many men, but he is always one step ahead of me.

He is new money. His grandfather gained a fortune in Hollywood that his descendants don't seem to appreciate, given the way Odin lounges on my leather sofa - legs spread wide and without dignity.

He takes a puff of his cigar. "I like you, Jerome."

"For you, I am the Marquis."

"Pardonne-mois, Monsieur le Marquis." He mocks me.

I clench my jaw so tightly that it almost pops out of my face. Leech.

"I don't have much time, Odin. Get to the point." A glance at my watch tells me that I am already late. I hate lateness like the plague.

"Don't tell me you have a date."

Sometimes I wonder how this man hasn't squandered his inheritance completely. He is undisciplined, self-absorbed, and greedy. But then again, he has excellent intuition and his ruthless nature has brought him to where he is today. In the cigar room of my estate.

"As you surely know, I am engaged. I have

obligations," I say.

"A little bird might have whispered it to me, yes," Odin replies. I want to smack the arrogance off his bloated face.

"Honestly, I never took you for a man who could be tied down. Weren't you always a playboy?" Odin takes a sip of his drink. He enjoys my expensive whiskey.

"That you don't understand doesn't surprise me," I say in a hoarse voice. I haven't slept much lately. "Your world is not like mine. You're content with expensive cars and watches. In my circles, different values matter. We are a closely-knit community that values tradition and trust. A name carries more weight than mere pleasure. But why am I wasting my breath? The doors to power will always remain closed to you."

Odin is on the verge of grabbing me by the collar and slamming me against the nearest wall.

"True power," I emphasize.

He empties his glass in one gulp.

"Where is Roman?"

His face turns pale. "You know he's gone missing. I can't tell you where he is at the moment. Probably fucking around on some island, snorting away my money."

"Until he resurfaces, our business dealings are on hold."

Odin jumps up. The glass slips from his hand and shatters into a thousand pieces. "You wouldn't dare."

"Roman is the only reason I'm even talking to you. He should call me if he's still alive. Then we'll talk further."

Odin's mouth hangs open. I laugh at him. As the door closes behind me, it's seventeen minutes past eight. For the first time in my life, I am late.

Louise isn't wearing a bra. Why the hell isn't she wearing a bra?

I train six times a week, wake up at 4:30 every morning, and take care of every inch of my body with dedication. I wait patiently when my enemies provoke me, never rushing into anything, and can suppress a feeling for years before taking action.

I am a disciplined man, but Louise's hard nipples beneath the delicate fabric of her dress push me to the limits of self-control.

I must not look. Determinedly, I cut into the meat. Take a sip of my wine… and glance over.

Firm and begging to be touched by me, they pierce through the pale pink silk. My pants begin to tighten. I clear my throat.

"The lamb is excellent," I manage to say through clenched teeth.

Madame de Guise blushes. She has a weakness for me. "We had it slaughtered just for you."

Louise wrinkles her nose and shoots a meaningful glance at her sister. I don't like them as a pair.

By herself, my fiancée is reserved and quiet (minus the unfortunate incident in my piano room), but as soon as her sister is around, cheeky remarks slip off her tongue more easily.

It doesn't matter. In a few weeks, everyone sitting at the table tonight will be dead. Including Louise.

The family has invited me for dinner as a way to make amends for Louise trying to break off our engagement. Since I walked through the door, she hasn't even glanced at me once.

I feel nothing for her, but her little hard nipples are driving me insane.

"Will your mother be present at the wedding?"

Madame de Guise knows no other topic than this cursed wedding day. I have tried to steer the conversation towards other, more interesting subjects, like the precious clocks on the dining room wall or the latest political events in our world, but she always manages to bring it back to the wedding after just a few sentences.

"No," I reply with a composed voice. "Madame de Colbert is ill with a lung disease and no longer goes out in public."

An uncomfortable silence settles over us. I despise pity.

Charlotte can't resist making a remark. "Then who will be your guest of honor… Monsieur Marquis?"

The irony in her words is unmistakable. I know what she's getting at, and I don't spare her the pain of my honest answer.

"Madison Reese."

Silence hangs in the air. No one says a word. I look

up from Louise's nipples to her face. She is flushed bright red.

Poor thing. I will have to teach her how to hide her emotions better.

I take the last piece of lamb into my mouth. I've been here for two hours. Just about thirty more minutes, and then I will finally apologize myself.

"How can you be so fixated on good manners on one hand and be such an asshole on the other?"

I choke on my own saliva. Louise rises from her chair. The pink silk caresses her delicate body.

"If you think I will allow your lover to be present at my wedding, you are mistaken. That will only happen over my dead body."

She pushes her chair back and heads towards the door. "Literally." And she's gone.

It is rare for me to lose composure. I don't know problems, only strategies. But I am unfamiliar with the mood swings of a twenty-something girl. Her mother looks at me.

"I am so sorry, I will bring her back so she can apologize to you, I…"

My lips move on their own. "Don't worry. I will go after her."

TEN

My footsteps echo through the corridor. I will pack my things and disappear. Change my name, invent a new one, and leave it all behind. I am nothing to him.

A strong hand grabs my shoulder from behind, throwing me off balance. A shrill scream escapes my throat. The hand moves to cover my mouth, cutting off my air supply. An arm wraps around my shoulders. I am trapped.

"Shh…" a deep voice whispers in my ear. "Not a peep. You will listen to me now."

I would recognize the scent of the Marquis anywhere. He smells like forgotten fairy tales that went extinct because they were too cruel to tell to children.

His arm holds me so tightly that I have no chance of breaking free from his grasp. He is only inches away from my breasts…

"I do you a favor, and instead of being grateful, you mock my generosity?"

Hopefully, Charlotte needs to use the restroom and passes by us. Someone has to help me. His large body presses against mine from behind. He is a giant.

"I don't want to hurt you. You're young and… inexperienced. But there's one thing you should have understood by now - I don't appreciate disrespect.

Your public outbursts end now. You have raised your voice against me for the last time. Is that clear?"

I can't speak, he still presses his hand against my lips. A tear runs down my face. Breathlessly, I nod.

"Good." He releases me. I gasp for air. I can't believe what just happened.

He looks down at me. "Show me what a good girl you can be, Louise."

The tears won't stop. "I can't."

He crosses his arms over his chest.

"Explain."

"I can't just throw my life away like that. I know that your promise will save me, but the thought of all those years in your castle, without warmth, without someone to hold me and tell me that everything will be okay no matter what… I can't do it."

I look up at him, seeking help. He is intelligent. Experienced in life. He could give me advice, a caring word that helps me keep my head above water. He takes a deep breath.

"You have your father to thank for all of this. Spare me your tears and cry to him instead. You will have to come to terms with the fact that from now on, you belong to me. Whether you want to or not."

Where his heart should be, there is a deep abyss leading straight to hell.

"How many people have you killed?" The words burst uncontrollably from me. "Will you kill me too once I am no longer useful to you?"

A shadow flickers across his face, so quickly that

I'm not sure if I really saw it.

"I will turn around now, return to your family, and pretend as if nothing happened - and you will do the same. Do you understand?"

When I don't respond, he grabs my wrist and pulls me along behind him towards the dining room.

He won't have the opportunity to kill me. I will get to him first and cut off his dick.

ELEVEN
The Marquis

Madison is the most beautiful woman I ever slept with.

I gaze out the window as she sucks my dick. Her soft moans fade behind a wall of fatigue and restlessness.

Fatigue, as I haven't slept all night. Restlessness, because Louise is getting on my last nerve. It was supposed to be easy. A signature, a promise, a wedding. She gets an expensive ring on her finger and keeps her mouth shut.

Unfortunately, I underestimated Louise. She's stronger than she appears at first glance, and I like that.

Madison pushes my cock deeper into her throat. It's getting harder.

Louise's nipples...

I bury my fingers in her blonde hair and pull her forward. A strange gurgling sound escapes from her mouth as I cum inside her. She swallows everything. She loves every part of me.

Madison smiles at me. "That was fun."

I don't know what to say in response. Lately, my mind has been filled with chaos. Normally, I'd put her on my desk and fuck her brains out. But I don't feel like it.

"I think I'm getting sick," I clear my throat and zip up my pants.

"Do you have a fever?" She places a concerned hand on my forehead, a well-intentioned gesture that only makes me feel worse.

"I just feel nauseous," I reply.

She grins. "I told you not to have dinner with those clowns."

"They're not clowns, darling. They belong to one of the oldest families in France - and we both know you fucked your way up from Brooklyn, so you better keep your sweet mouth shut if you don't know what you're talking about."

She's used to me. Sometimes I wonder why she even stays by my side. Then I remember that I hold a title and lead the Circle, and everything makes sense.

If my response hurts her, she doesn't show it. She's a master of charades.

"Speaking of them, how long do you plan on keeping this act up? Everyone knows your marriage will be a farce. Aren't you embarrassed to lie to the faces of people who know the truth?", she says, slipping back into her dress now that it's obvious I won't satisfy her tonight.

Hurt pride emanates from her. I place a thumb under her chin and run my index finger along her lower lip. "Have patience, darling. Give me a year, and this charade will be over."

She has never been satisfied with brief answers She always wants to know the whole story.

"You're going to get a divorce? Are you aware that it's the biggest shame you could bring upon your family name?"

I wave it off. I'm tired. "No. Gino will take care of it."

"Gino? My Gino?"

"Exactly. I promised him that he'll be allowed to kill Louise after a year has passed. He'll make it look like a tragic accident."

A malicious grin spreads across Madison's face.

"I'd be lying if I said I didn't like that." She steps closer to me and breathes in my ear. "Just promise me one thing. When she's dead – let me see her body. I want to spit in her face one last time."

Perhaps she is only the second most beautiful woman I've met.

TWELVE

My father always works late into the night at the library. Our shared love for books is what connects us. Nothing more.

He wasn't there when I took my first steps, and he cheated on Mother with his secretary while I celebrated my graduation.

Albert is just a shadow to me, a vague idea of what a father could be. I don't remember a single hug.

The light is still on. I know he's desperately searching for ways to free himself from Gino's grip. Even though the door is slightly ajar, I knock.

Albert looks up from the documents he's working on. "Louise. You're still awake?"

It has been two weeks since the disastrous dinner with the Marquis, and Mother still hasn't forgiven me for my behaviour. Albert has long forgotten about it. "Come in, little one."

I hesitantly follow his invitation, even though that's why I came - to talk to him and ask him the questions that weigh on my soul.

I sit down on one of the chairs across from him.

"What is it?"

With his mustache and round glasses, he looks so harmless, but appearances can be deceiving.

My father may be leaner than the Marquis and

three heads shorter, but he has no less blood on his hands than my fiancé.

In our world, no one is innocent. I wonder if one day I will lose my innocence as well. Not through sex. Through betrayal. The innocence of my heart.

"Are you making progress?" I ask.

"I suppose you could say that. Our summer estate in the Provence has found a potential buyer, and I am currently working on a proposal to…"

"That's not what I'm talking about."

He knows exactly what I mean - where I'm heading with this. "Have you found a solution to our problem?"

Two years ago, Albert traveled to Palermo with his secretary to forget, for a duration of two weeks, that he had a family and obligations.

Unfortunately, he crossed paths with Gino, the oldest member of the Circle. They had never been friends - and when Gino told my father about a deal that was about to be finalized, Albert intervened.

He tried to get ahead of Gino and persuade the men working for him to join his side. Unsuccessfully. All it brought him was the anger of a stronger opponent and his consequent demise.

A man like Gino never forgets. He wants to erase our name, even if it's the last thing he does.

"My child, these things are too big for you. You wouldn't understand."

"I understand that my sister's life is at stake. That's all I need to know. So tell me, have you found a solution?"

His silence says it all.

"I have an idea."

He listens. At least I have his undivided attention, without my overzealous mother interrupting. That's a good start.

"I will ask the Marquis to arrange a match for Charlotte."

Albert gasps. "You will not do that. Don't you dare."

"Why?"

"Because we have already shown him enough weakness. He knows that we rely on him, and even if... we come out of this alive, he will forever use this defeat against us. If he saves Charlotte's life, we will owe him an additional favor and be bound to him."

"I can't believe it." My hands grip the table. "Your damn honor is more important to you than your own daughter's life."

My vision goes black.

"As I said before." Albert looks down in shame. "You are too young to understand."

Shaking my head, I stand up. "I understand the most important thing. This family is not a family, but just a group of randomly assembled strangers. You never loved Mother - and you don't love your own children either."

He jumps up.

"How can you even think such a thing, let alone say it?"

"Let's leave it at that."

I'm already out the door when I add, "Whatever fate awaits me at the Marquis's, it can't be sadder than life under this roof - and whether you like it or not, I will save Charlotte. Whatever it takes."

THIRTEEN

The Marquis is sick. He refuses to admit that he's unwell, but I can see it in his feverish face. He sweats and shivers at the same time as he receives me in his study, where painted angels from the 18th century gaze down at us from the rounded ceiling. His castle is a gilded cage.

A selection of desserts sits on his desk, and he alternates between them while he speaks.

"I have a proposal for you, Louise."

A bit of cream sticks to his upper lip. My gaze lingers on it. He notices and slowly licks it away. *Focus!*

"I'm all ears."

He smiles, but it's a weak smile. He's worse off than he wants to admit. As he begins to speak, his lungs start to wheeze, and he's interrupted by a fit of coughing.

"If you want my honest opinion..." I start, but he cuts me off with a gesture.

"Not today."

"You shouldn't be working. You need bed rest and sleep."

I can see him holding his breath to suppress a cough. "I'm fine. I never get sick."

"Of course."

He shoots me a dark look across the table.

"Louise…"

"Alright, alright. I'm listening."

His Adam's apple twitches. For a split second, I get lost in the sight of his broad shoulders and the bicep that stretches his tailored suit to its limits.

"I would like to move the wedding forward."

I furrow my brow suspiciously. "Why?"

"It fits better into my schedule."

"All of a sudden?"

"Yes, all of a sudden. Economic developments and business relationships aren't always predictable."

I smell bullshit, but he's not a man who easily gives away his secrets.

"Fine by me," I shrug as nonchalantly as possible.

He seems relieved. Today, it's harder for him to hide his true feelings because the flu weakens him.

"On one condition," I add.

His relief dissipates into thin air. "And what would that be?" he asks.

"I want you to set up Charlotte with one of your friends."

His jaw twitches. The Marquis is eleven years older than me, and I'm sure he could teach me things I don't even dare to imagine. *Louise!* I want to slap myself on the forehead to punish myself for my thoughts. *Don't forget that this will be a marriage of convenience.*

"No," his voice fills the room.

"Yes." I push my chin forward.

"Never."

I have no choice. I have to bluff...

"Alright. Then we'll get married in two and a half months, as originally planned."

Slowly and deliberately, I stand up from my chair and walk towards the door.

One, two...

"Wait!"

I knew it.

"Sit down."

With an innocent face, I comply with his order. I can be obedient - if I want to.

"Does it matter which friend I choose for her?"

"No. The main thing is that she's safe from Gino's people."

I can't explain why I'm entrusting my sister's life to the Marquis.

"Then it's settled. We'll marry at the beginning of next month." His commanding tone sends shivers down my spine. I swallow hard. So soon... "Agreed."

We shake hands. He holds onto me for one breath too long. His warmth seeps into me. His thumb teases my skin with a gentle stroke.

His eyes hold me captive.

"I like my women submissive and obedient. Will you be able to remember that, Louise?"

My hand is paralyzed. I can't move anymore. He misinterprets my silence.

"Wonderful. You may leave."

FOURTEEN
The Marquis

I almost feel sorry for her, and I despise myself for it. Her eyes are so full of hope. She looks at me, and I can see in her face that she overestimates the goodness in me.

She wants to believe that I will use my power to protect her fragile heart from dying. She looks at me, hoping that my cold demeanor is just a mask that I will drop if she gives me enough time. If she gets to know me better.

A bitter taste settles on my tongue. Something tightens within me. My special gift is being able to guess the weaknesses of others with closed eyes. Her ability to dream will be her downfall. Her belief that everyone can change will kill her.

All of this, I read on her lips without her having to say it out loud.

Louise closes the door behind her. Her steps are so soft that I can no longer hear them after a few seconds.

She fell for it. If I had known it would be so easy, I wouldn't have put in as much effort. I am aware that our wedding planner will personally tear my head off, but it's worth it. I need to rid myself of this burden. There are more important things demanding my attention.

A NOBLE CONTRACT

Ever since I got engaged to Louise de Guise, everything revolves around dresses, cakes, and empty promises. Her family clings to me like a squashed insect. Fatigue has taken hold of my bones. I haven't had a full night's sleep in weeks.

This girl is driving me crazy. If we marry sooner, less time will pass before a year has gone by and Gino can take care of what I should handle myself.

Louise will die. The sooner, the better.

FIFTEEN

Everything in me begs the gods that no one will die at my wedding.

It's not uncommon for one of the guests to fall backwards from their chair at grand celebrations. Poisoned wine, poisoned cake - I have seen it all.

My uncle died at my parents' wedding celebration. Someone stabbed him from behind during the ceremony and was never captured.

The type of people who attend our festivities have a weakness for theatrical gestures. Public executions are considered good manners.

Air escapes my lungs as my mother pulls tighter on the lacing of the dress chosen for me by the Marquis. I was allowed to choose between two fabric options, but he decided everything else.

The dress is conservative. It covers my arms and half of my neck completely. I also have to wear gloves. The message is clear. *You belong to me, and no one else is allowed to look at you.*

"Tighter, please," I gasp. "I can still breathe."

"How funny." My mother is in a milder mood today than usual. She hasn't scolded me once.

"I wouldn't want me to make it to the altar without fainting first, would I?"

She ignores my remark and tightens the laces even more. I'm sure I'm already turning blue underneath the dress.

Charlotte is applying lipstick. Lilac-colored, like the thousands of flowers that fill the wedding hall. The Marquis has spared no expense.

"Have you seen his suit?" I ask her.

She winks at me in the mirror. "Oh, yes. Let me just say this - you won't be disappointed when you free him from his pants tonight."

The fact that my mother doesn't scold her for her comment shows how nervous she is. Satisfied, she stands in front of me and gives me a smile.

"You look beautiful. I'm so proud of you, Louise."

She grabs my shoulders and pushes me in front of the floor-to-ceiling mirror in my dressing room.

It's true. I look stunning. My hair is perfectly curled up and the makeup artist has highlighted my features flawlessly. I've never seen myself like this before.

"Not bad, big sister," Charlotte pinches my cheek. "The Marquis will definitely get excited when he sees you."

I blush. "Fine by me. Either way, nothing will happen between us."

My mother's smile freezes. "What are you intending?"

Talking to your own parents about sex ranks right after arranged marriage with a murderer on the list of uncomfortable things.

"I'm not going to sleep with him."

Her eyes darken. "Oh, my dear, you will."

Outraged, I try to turn around to face her, but she tightly grips my shoulders.

"Isn't it enough that you've ruined our lives and forced me into an unhappy marriage? Now you want to decide what I do with my body, too?"

She presses her thin lips together. "You know the rules. A marriage is only valid if it is consummated."

My eyes are about to fall back into my head from how forcefully I roll them.

"Maybe 300 years ago."

"300 years ago and today. Traditions keep our world alive. They are not meant to be changed, but followed. The Marquis is a man of old-fashioned values. He will deflower you, and you will allow it."

Acid starts to gather in my mouth. "Disgusting. I will *not* sleep with him. I'd rather die."

Charlotte takes my hand reassuringly and leads me towards the limousine.

The Marquis insisted on a church wedding. His family presents themselves as strict Catholics, which I can only laugh at considering the many deaths they are responsible for.

We marry in a small village behind Versailles, near his castle. He has chosen the church where he was baptized as a newborn. It is neither remarkably pompous nor breathtakingly beautiful, but it holds sentimental value for him.

His family has been married here for centuries.

The limousine stops, and I spot no soul in sight.

No one smilingly waiting for me or offering words of encouragement.

Charlotte steps out of the car. "Good luck." She kisses my forehead and disappears through a side entrance.

Don't forget to breathe. You can do this. It's just one day in your entire life, and in five years, you'll look back on this day and be able to laugh about it. Hopefully.

It feels strange to walk towards the church alone. My train is dragging me down, and my veil is making it difficult for me to see.

As I spot Albert at the entrance after a few meters, I breathe a sigh of relief. He kisses my hand. Since our argument in the library, we haven't seen each other, but I'm glad he's here, grateful that I don't have to walk this path alone.

"You will always be my beloved daughter, no matter what happens," he whispers in my ear, and the music starts playing before I can tell him that he will always have a place in my heart despite everything. That I love him.

The doors open. I see him immediately. His graceful posture and handsome face outshine all the other guests.

He's facing my direction, looking into my eyes. There are several meters between us, but in the dim light of the church windows, he is the anchor, the future, the salvation for me and my sister.

I have to trust a man I don't know. I have no other choice.

In rhythm with the music, I take one step after another. The strong arm of my father supports me.

The Marquis is wearing a perfectly tailored cream-colored ensemble. A brooch showing the Colbert family crest adorns his chest.

He watches my every move. He lurks. As I come to a stop in front of the altar, he looks down at me from above.

His perfect face is an unfathomable ocean.

Albert takes a deep breath. "Take good care of her. I beg you."

The Marquis responds with a brief nod. He reaches out his hand to me. I let go of my father. My fingers reach towards him. He envelops them with a touch so gentle that I wouldn't have expected from him.

One, two, three steps up the stairs. For the duration of a brief eternity, I lose myself in the infinite depths of his eyes. The priest starts to speak, but I can barely hear him.

„"In good times and in bad... until death do you part."

The Marquis takes a deep breath. The priest hands him the red velvet cushion with our rings on it. He brings my hand closer to him.

"I do."

I am his.

"I do."

Forever bound to him.

"You may now kiss the bride."

I feel a chill run through me. A rushing sound fills my ears. This moment of the ceremony should not be a surprise to me. I knew what would happen, and yet everything in me tenses up.

The Marquis lightly touches the tulle of my veil with his fingertips. Slowly, he lifts it up. He leans forward ever so slightly. His head wanders towards my ear.

"You are beautiful," he whispers so softly that only my heart can hear it… and he places his lips on mine. Soft and warm. A promise that he will hide me in his fortress and protect me with his life.

I gasp for air. He's everywhere. Seconds pass. The kiss lingers. Too long. A guest coughs.

The Marquis releases me and straightens his tie. Am I mistaken, or are his cheeks flushed? He doesn't look at me.

The crowd begins to applaud as he takes my hand and pulls me towards the exit. White flower petals rain down on us. A warm feeling rises in my chest. Maybe everything can still be alright.

Suddenly the Marquis seems to be in a hurry. He grabs my shoulders and pushes me towards the door. My heel gets caught in the hem of my dress. I stumble forward. He grabs my hips. I float a meter above the ground.

A deafening bang cuts through the air. Everything inside me tightens. I scream in panic.

The Marquis pushes me forward, outside, away from the crowd that starts to roar and my mother's distorted face.

I can't breathe anymore. This is my end.

"Let go of me," I scream. "I have to go back. I have to be with him."

The Marquis says nothing. He grabs the back of my neck and forces me onto the backseat of his car.

"Go!" he yells so loudly that my heart skips a beat. The driver starts moving.

I see nothing but the images that will haunt me forever from now on. My father's limp body. My mother's bloody hands. Albert is dead. Someone shot him.

SIXTEEN

The Marquis

It had to happen. We all knew that Albert was destined to die - but I don't appreciate the fact that Gino chose the day of my wedding to seek revenge. It's a clear message: *remember your promise, Marquis. Louise will die.*

She trembles in my arms. Her whole body shakes as she's overwhelmed by one sob after another.

I saw the shooter before he pulled the trigger. The only thing I could do was guide my bride towards the exit and pull her out of the line of fire. The rest was out of my hands.

Her little fingers cling to my thigh. I have never felt so helpless in my entire life.

I always know what to do.

I always have a plan, but Louise's tears on the fabric of my suit paralyze me.

It's not her father's death that shocks me. It's her arms clinging to me, her face hiding against my chest. It's the trust with which she seeks shelter in me. She doesn't know who she's dealing with.

"Take me to him," she begs, her voice so weak it turns my stomach. She looks up at me, her face full of tears. Her perfectly applied mascara is ruined.

I can't explain what has come over me but my hand moves as if guided by someone else, reaching for her face and my thumb begins to stroke her cheek.

"There's nothing we could do. He's dead."

She starts hyperventilating. I hold her tighter against my chest.

"They won't hurt you. You're safe with me."

Her phone rings. She's so trapped in her trance that she doesn't even hear it. Her sister's name lights up on the display. I answer on Louise's behalf.

"Yes?"

"Where is Louise?"

"She's safe."

"I want to talk to her."

"No. She's not in a condition to speak."

"I. Want. To. Talk. To her."

Hot anger makes the hairs on the back of my neck stand up.

"In case you missed it, and if your sister's wedding dress wasn't clue enough - she is now my wife. I will decide what's best for her, and right now she needs rest. She will contact you as soon as she's in a condition to do so."

Without waiting for a response, I end the call.

Louise has fallen asleep in my arms, exhausted. I look out the window. This is all too dangerous. Not just for her. But for me as well.

SEVENTEEN

Everything spins. The world is a black abyss, and I can't breathe.

I awake with a loud scream. My heart races in my chest. The window is wide open. Cold wind brushes against my face.

I'm in my new bedroom. The Marquis must have laid me on the bed while I slept. I'm still wearing my wedding dress.

A gentle clearing of a throat makes me flinch. A young woman around my age stands in the corner of the room. She's wearing a uniform and has her arms crossed behind her back.

"May I bring you something to drink, Madame?"

Her red hair and countless freckles on her face are visible even in the darkness of the night. Her warm smile offers me some solace, if only a little.

"Please."

She nods, approaches me, and pours sparkling water into a glass. I empty it in one gulp.

"Where is the Marquis?" I ask her.

"In his study. Shall I call him?"

I hastily shake my head. "No, please don't. What's your name?"

"Lola."

"Beautiful name. I like it."

I am paralyzed. I don't know how my life is

supposed to go on. My father. Dead. Covered in blood in my mother's arms.

"Should I leave you alone?" Her warm gaze settles on me.

"Can you stay with me? Only if you have nothing else to do."

"Of course. As long as you want."

"But please, have a seat."

Her confused expression tells me that the Marquis' staff usually stand in his presence. She hesitates, but eventually complies with my request and sinks into one of the pale yellow armchairs.

We don't speak a word. Her presence is a silent comfort to me, exactly what I need in these lonely moments. The clock on the wall completes two full rounds. It's almost ten o'clock when I hear footsteps on the stairs. The door opens without a knock.

The shadow of the Marquis appears, imposing and dark.

"How is she?" he asks Lola.

"Better than a few hours ago."

"Good. You can leave."

I straighten up. "No. I want her to stay."

I've only known Lola for two hours, but I already feel connected to her. She seems honest and loyal.

The Marquis puts both hands in the pockets of his suit. He hasn't changed clothes since the ceremony. Normally, we would have had a celebration to honor our union, with dances, well-wishes, and countless hugs. Instead, there is now a funeral to organize. He looks down at me.

"I don't think you want her here. Or am I mistaken about your preferences? I'm open to anything."

Was that an attempt at a joke? Lola shyly squeezes past him, and we're alone.

"What do you mean?"

"You know exactly what I mean. Stand up."

When I don't move, he gently grabs my arm and pulls me up towards him. My face is at the level of his chest.

"What are you doing?"

With both hands, I try to push him away from me. He doesn't budge an inch.

"We are now husband and wife."

"Only on paper."

"Even on paper, a marriage is only valid once it has been consummated," he turns away from me and walks towards the windows. His perfectly formed silhouette stands out against the darkness of the night.

His broad back moves as he says, "Undress."

I hope I misheard him.

"I won't ask you twice. Undress."

My hands clench into fists. "After everything that has happened today, can't you give me a small break?"

He turns to face me. His gaze is so dark and cold, so full of unspoken threats that I understand them all too well, leaving my words stuck in my throat.

With trembling fingers, I open my dress. It's too

tight.

"I… I don't know…"

He strides towards me with long steps. "Turn around."

I silently obey his command. With practiced hands, he loosens the lacing of my dress. The sound of heavy fabric slowly falling to the floor and his breath blowing on my neck is all I hear.

He doesn't speak. I am left wearing only my white lace underwear. He remains fully dressed.

Silently, he takes a step back and then begins to slowly circle around me. His intense gaze burns on my skin. We bathe in moonlight.

"Take off your bra," he comes so close to me that I can feel his breath. "I want to see what I've bought."

A hot sensation tingles between my thighs. It must be the fear of all the things he could do to me without anyone outside these four walls ever finding out.

Reluctantly, I let the bra straps slide off my shoulders and unclasp it at the back. He doesn't blink once. His full attention is on me.

"Good girl," his voice sounds rough and dangerous.

The bra falls to the floor. Cold air touches my breasts, and I feel the skin around my nipples tighten.

"Look at me." It takes all of my courage to lift my gaze.

We lock eyes. His handsome face is a mask, revealing nothing of what he thinks or feels.

"Go on."

Without taking my eyes off him, I slip out of the lace thong.

He steps even closer to me. I can see the hardness in his pants. Oh. God. Never. He's way too big for me.

He puts the index and middle fingers of his right hand together and touches my stomach. My breath catches in my throat. I've never been touched in this way by a man. My nipples are hard.

His burning gaze grows hungrier. He bites his lower lip and suddenly, with a single swift movement, he slides between my legs.

A moan escapes my throat and I feel ashamed of it.

"Mmmh," he growls. "So wet for me."

I close my eyes. A thousand unfamiliar emotions overwhelm me all at once.

"It seems that your body doesn't hate me as much as your heart does."

I feel dizzy from the deep timbre of his voice.

His thumb moves to my mouth and slips between my lips.

"Louise." The green of his eyes swallows me. I am so vulnerable right now.

"Everything - your chambers, my vows, the kiss at the altar - it's all a lie." His signet ring, bearing the crest of the Circle, gleams in the moonlight.

"I took you as my wife to settle a debt, but I will never be your husband." He releases his grip. "Our connection is purely business. Don't you ever forget that."

My face burns with all-consuming shame. I close my eyes, and when I open them again, he is gone. In all my 21 years, I have never felt so small and insignificant.

EIGHTEEN

The scraping of cutlery on porcelain plates hurts my ears. Usually, I can always eat. Today, the macarons and petit fours get stuck in my throat.

The Marquis has a weakness for sweets. His way of breakfasting will soon give me cavities and five kilos more on my hips.

He watches me from the other end of the long table as I poke at the pastry with my fork.

"Shall I have eggs prepared for you?"

I don't respond.

"Croissants? Cheese? Champagne?"

My offended gaze bounces off him. In public, in front of important men and under the gaze of his servants, he presents himself as an old school gentleman. Behind closed doors, he slides between my legs and mocks me.

"I'm not hungry."

"But you should eat. After everything that happened yesterday."

I exhale loudly through my nose.

"Since when do you care about my well-being?"

"I don't. It's well-intentioned advice."

Since Albert… passed away, I haven't spoken to Charlotte. I need to call her, but before that, I need answers. This isn't about my wounded pride, it's about her and the help she needs.

"Have you found a potential fiance for my sister?"

The question catches him off guard. He takes a sip of his coffee. No matter what he does, his movements are elegant and intimidating. Every smile, every gesture conveys that the world belongs to him and we are his puppets.

I have never dared to ask myself, what the Chairman of the Circle actually does. I know he's influential and brings together the men who determine the course of humanity. But I can't even begin to imagine what exactly this work looks like.

I wonder if he's in danger. If a rival would eliminate him to take his position.

"You must have patience, Louise." My hand clenches into a fist.

"Patience? My father was shot in front of my eyes yesterday. And I'm supposed to wait until the next member of my family is targeted? Would you like to offer me another cup of tea to pass the time?"

Determined, I push my chair back and approach my... husband.

"When I agreed to move the wedding forward, it was under one condition. Even though you are older than me, your memory can't be that bad, can it?"

His mouth twitches, whether with anger or amusement, I cannot tell.

"That is why you will listen to me carefully now, Monsieur le Marquis." I make a great effort to put all my contempt into his title.

"I am fed up with being used by wealthy men in

sophisticated suits. I am a human being, with dreams and emotions. With a past and a future. The game that you believe you play so masterfully ends here and now. You will help me."

The Marquis leans back in his chair and looks at me amusedly from head to toe.

"Most people beg for my help on their knees, but you demand it. I like that." Before I know it, his fingers are intertwined with mine.

"I will call every single one of my eligible friends today. We shall see what can be done."

NINETEEN

The air smells of winter. Six weeks have passed since my father's death, and the trees have shed their leaves. Everything is withered.

The funeral proceeds quietly. Fewer friends have come than expected. A life filled with empty promises and fake smiles did not bring happiness to my father.

Mother is not the same anymore. She has completely collapsed after his death. I never thought I would miss her admonitions and sharp comments, but as a silent tear falls from her cheeks onto the snow, I know that I have lost her forever.

My sister shows no emotion. Dressed in black from head to toe, she stands at Albert's grave, clutching a white rose. When it's time to say our final goodbyes, she lets the blossom fall onto his casket without a word.

The Marquis has organized the funeral. He knew that my mother would not be capable of doing so after her loss and took control.

He stands close beside me. Though we are strangers, I am grateful for his presence. He is a strong pillar in the storm. His hands are clad in black leather gloves, and when I momentarily feel myself faltering, my knees weakening, they rest on my lower back. I shudder under his touch. Everything about him exudes confidence and strength.

I shouldn't forget that he's only by my side to prevent any gossip about us. He fulfills his marital obligations in public.

Behind closed doors, what Madison had predicted has come true. Even after weeks of living together, the Marquis hardly acknowledges my presence most days, ignoring my questions and shutting down any attempts at conversation.

We eat in silence, we sleep in separate beds, and at night I hear Madison's moans from his chambers.

I do not want to play the role of his wife, but a friend would be welcome during these difficult times. He has traveled extensively, seen every corner of this world, while I know nothing beyond France. If he wanted to, he could alleviate some of my sadness by telling me about the beautiful places on this planet.

But I am insignificant to him.

He supports me with one arm as we silently make our way towards his car.

Charlotte embraces me tighter than ever before.

"I love you," she whispers.

Every goodbye could be our last.

"Dane Gilbertson, an old college friend of mine, has agreed to meet with Charlotte."

I turn my gaze away from the passing snowy landscape and look at the Marquis sitting beside me in the backseat.

"Really?"

"Really. But don't get your hopes up too high, he's

not really looking for a wife yet. But when I explained your... situation to him, I must have miraculously touched his stone-cold heart. He's willing to hear you out and - if Charlotte appeals to him - consider a marriage."

A wave of excitement sweeps over me, carrying me away and causing me to throw myself into his arms. I wrap my arms around him. He stiffens under my touch. We find ourselves in an awkward position, half sitting, half lying down, with all my weight on him and his muscles as hard as stone.

"Thank you, thank you, thank you," I exclaim in a high-pitched tone. His breath tickles my neck as he chuckles softly. I was certain he sold his smile to the devil.

"I will never forget about this."

As he still doesn't move, I slowly pull away from him. His cheeks are tinged with a light pink color. If I didn't know any better, I could believe he's embarrassed.

I beam with joy as I fall back onto my side of the backseat.

"Don't get too excited," he says in a rough voice. He runs a hand through his perfectly gelled hair, which now stands in all directions after our embrace.

"It's just an attempt, and I can't promise you that he will actually agree to it." He reaches for my hand, and his touch freezes me, the sensation of his skin against mine.

"Dane suggested that we meet. The four of us.

Tomorrow." His searching gaze penetrates every corner of my heart. "Would that be okay with you? I know today was your father's funeral, and…"

He falls silent as I can no longer hold back and press a grateful kiss to his cheek. His skin smells masculine and warm. Although he is perfectly shaved, I feel a hint of his stubble against my lips.

"I thank you. From the bottom of my heart. It's not true what people say about you. You have a good heart."

I tap him on the chest. "Even if you hide it well."

His whole demeanor changes. He suddenly appears soft and vulnerable, his face younger, more hopeful.

As if he can read my thoughts, he quickly turns his head and looks out the window. For the first time since we've been together, the silence between us is not uncomfortable.

TWENTY
The Marquis

Madison wants a child with me. We have never discussed starting a family in the past.

Naturally, I must father a successor. A son. But I always pushed this thought away into an uncertain, distant future.

Madison is not the woman to maintain my bloodline. To be honest, I can't imagine ever finding in a woman what it takes to bring a Colbert into the world.

We're destructive.

I have never told her I loved her. Because I'm incapable of love. My life has always had one purpose: to rule. I'm not the man who cuddles with a woman, holds her hand when she cries, and promises to fulfill her dreams.

I need rough, dirty sex and the feeling of not being completely alone in this merciless world.

Madison has convinced herself that she loves me, but she has tied her heart to my wealth. To the carefree lifestyle she enjoys by my side as we jet from one paradise to another, and I adorn her with diamonds around her neck. Our connection has always been casual for me.

In our circles, there were whispers that we were secretly engaged, and I know that Madison believes

Louise took what rightfully belonged to her. But for me, it has always been a game.

One that I don't seem to have played well enough, because now Madison is sitting in front of me on the edge of my bed, looking at me begging.

"No matter how many tears you cry, I won't change my mind. I don't want a child with you."

I never lied to her. She always knew what she was getting into.

"Is it because of her? Do you like her?"

Her face turns crimson. I fasten the cufflinks with my family crest on them. *Don't let her provoke you*, I remind myself.

"If you believe that, then you know me worse than I thought."

She rises from the bed and approaches me. She's beautiful. Our sex is unique. But she has never touched my heart. No one has ever found a way to do so.

Her hands rest on my chest.

"Why don't you take me with you then? We haven't been out together in so long."

The black dress I gifted her hugs her curves perfectly. Strangely, her appearance doesn't arouse me today. I have other things on my mind. An important evening lies ahead of me.

I've either suffered an undetected stroke or simply lost my mind, because I actually allowed myself to approach my friends at Louise's request.

What purpose does it serve to fulfill a promise

when everything is going to end soon anyway? Louise is going to die. Her sister cannot be saved.

Nevertheless, I managed to convince Dane to go out with us tonight. He doesn't really belong to my inner circle. We played golf together for a while, but he's a drinker who makes too many promises when he's bored. He's also the only one who was open to the idea of marrying a de Guise.

All the others fear Gino too much. No one has the power that I possess. Only I can protect a woman from him. Anyone else would be helpless against his wrath.

So why don't you protect Louise? Why do you expose her to him, even though she trusts you?

Because I don't owe her anything, damn it. She's a stranger.

Are you sure about that?

"It's not true what people say about you. You have a good heart."

I feel sick. Madison still looks at me expectantly, waiting for my answer.

"What was the question?"

She looks puzzled. I get why. I don't usually drift off like this.

"Why don't you take me with you? It would be a clear sign to the public. Everyone could see that you stand by me, even though you're married to that slut."

I grab her wrist. She recoils in shock.

"Don't talk about my wife like that."

We stand face to face, glaring at each other. There's a knock on the door. Endless seconds pass before I manage to break free from my angry trance and let go of Madison. I've never seen her so upset.

"Come in."

Louise peeks shyly through the crack in the door. "I'm ready."

"Come here."

I reach out to her. Suspicious, she follows my invitation.

"Let me take a look at you."

She steps in, and I catch my breath. Tomorrow, I'll call my neurologist immediately because now I'm sure that something is wrong with my nervous system. I have goosebumps.

"Is this okay? I wasn't sure if it looks boring…"

Her light green dress is nowhere near as tight-fitting as Madison's. In a healthy state, I could never find it appealing. But thanks to my questionable condition, it looks so breathtaking that I forget to swallow.

She blushes. "Is it that bad? I can go change."

"I think it's a lost cause," Madison replies for me. I'm going to kill her.

With all the remaining strength I have, I force myself to speak. "It's fine. We're already running late. Let's go."

My legs start moving, and I hear Louise and Madison silently following me. Louise is not used to walking in high heels, and she falls behind. I wait for her at the entrance door, holding her winter coat in both hands. She shyly lets me help her put it on.

Surprised, I turn to Madison as she grabs my wrist and holds me back. Louise is already out of earshot.

"I have no idea what game you're playing, Jerome. But don't underestimate me or you'll regret it. Do you understand?"

My jaw clenches. She tries to hold onto me with all her strength, but I effortlessly free myself from her grip.

"Don't forget who you are, Madison. I made you, and I can destroy you."

My words hurt her. Good.

Dane is waiting for us outside a club that I would never have chosen for this meeting.

I solely spend time in private locations, where strict admission procedures ensure that you only meet the people who will help you move forward in life.

Dane has opted for a nightclub in the heart of Paris, and it turns my stomach as we pull up in my car. Charlotte and Louise whisper behind me.

Today, I am driving myself. Miracles do happen.

The first warning sign: there's no one at the entrance checking who is on the guest list. Even worse, it seems like there is no guest list at all.

Dane is clearly already drunk. He greets me with a kiss on the cheek, and I make a mental note to sell all the shares I hold in his company tomorrow to diminish their value.

"Can I leave you alone for a moment? I need to park the car."

Warning sign number three. Public parking.

This is my punishment for letting Louise convince me into this half-baked plan.

"Of course." Dane's eyes gleam a little too much for my liking as he puts an arm around Louise and Charlotte, pulling them close to him. "You don't even have to come back, as far as I'm concerned."

Before I let myself be carried away by the idea of committing a public murder, I quickly get back into the car and park it as close as possible, which is still a half-hour walk away.

When I return to the location, there is no trace of any of them. This is starting off wonderfully.

Anger rises within me as the crowd doesn't part for me, and I have to push my way through sweaty bodies.

I may be an arrogant asshole, but my arrogance has gotten me to where I am today, and under normal circumstances, that does not involve having someone else's sweat sticking to my suit.

But since Louise entered my life, nothing has been normal anymore.

I take it all back. Public murder is completely acceptable. I will break his neck in three, two, one…

"There you are, Jerome!" Dane has placed his hand on my wife's lower back. Only the fantasy of showering that right hand with gasoline and accidentally dropping a match keeps me from immediately smashing his face in.

He has rented a lounge. Relief washes over me as a waiter opens the barrier and leads us into the VIP area. Under no circumstances will I mingle with the other guests and dance.

Louise is cut off by a group of hysterical women. Instinctively, I reach for her hand before she gets lost. Her nose twitches almost imperceptibly. By now, I know that happens whenever she feels embarrassed.

Two dark red, stained faux leather sofas are ours.

"How lovely." I don't even bother hiding my disgust.

Dane pats me on the shoulder in a friendly manner. "Relax, Jerome. Loosen up. Have some fun. If anyone needs it, it's you."

I've forgotten how unbearable he can be. But it's not about me. This evening is for Louise. For her sister. If I want to fulfill my promise, I have to hold back.

Whether I like it or not - Dane is doing me a favor, not the other way around.

We sit down. Louise takes a seat next to me. Her bare leg touches mine. I can feel the nervous heat of her skin through the fabric of my suit. She's afraid that the evening might not go as she hopes.

To calm her down, I lean back casually and place an arm behind her on the backrest. Her hair tickles my face as I lean towards her.

"Everything will be fine, Louise."

Goosebumps appear on her neck.

Dane orders the first round of champagne. When he pours the bottle over us ten minutes later, I remember why I don't associate with the nouveau riche.

But aside from my dislike of crowded places, everything seems to be going well. Charlotte sits across from us, close to Dane, and laughs. She's a damn good actress. Whatever he says, it can't be that funny.

"If you're not careful, the disgusted expression on your face will freeze eventually." Louise's lips glisten in the red light.

"Is that so?" I reply, half amused and half feigning disinterest.

"You could be handsome if you didn't constantly judge everyone around you," she says, clearly drunk.

Who would have thought she had such a low tolerance? Then again, it makes sense. The household she comes from definitely doesn't allow club visits for firstborn daughters, and her mother must have kept a close eye on how much her precious offspring drank at public events.

"I passionately enjoy keeping my distance from others."

Unlike Louise, I am still completely sober after three gin tonics.

A giggle escapes from between her full lips. "If you only knew what the women secretly call you behind your back."

She wants to provoke me - and it works. Innocently, her eyes wander back towards the dance floor. No one here knows my name. I have nothing to lose…

"What do they call me?"

Her words have piqued my curiosity, however she managed to do it. 300 years ago, she would have definitely been burned as a witch.

"Nope, sorry. Girl Code over everything. I won't tell you. You'll have to use your imagination a little…"

She beams at me triumphantly and takes a sip of her champagne. Every movement so innocent and yet so fatal.

I hold her gaze and lean closer in her direction.

Her hard nipples in the moonlight. My fingers between her wet thighs. She was surrendering herself to me…

My hand rests on her thigh. I have no clue how it ended up there. My fingers continue to wander upwards. A stifled breath escapes her throat.

Damn. It drives me crazy, the effect my touch has on her.

"If I wanted to, I could make you. You know I could. But…" - I withdraw my hand - "I'm a gentleman."

Before she has a chance to respond, my phone vibrates in my pocket. As the chairman of the Circle, I must be available at any time and in any place in the world. I don't know what it means to have time off.

"Please excuse me. I'll be right back."
Her cheeks are flushed. I thank the gods for saving me from a mistake I would have regretted forever.

The President's call has already been going on for twenty minutes. The matter could be resolved much faster if he didn't get lost in the details of his German Shepherd's illness.

Restlessly, I pace back and forth in the smoking area. I usually live for my work, but in this moment only one image occupies my mind: Dane motherfucking Gilbertson, with his dirty fingers touching my wife.

Your wife on paper.

Another seven minutes and fifty-eight seconds pass before we agree that I will go through the declaration of war that reached him tonight and work out a response strategy with him tomorrow morning.

My blood is boiling. Regardless of the consequences, I push aside anyone foolish enough to stand in my way.

My pulse normalizes as Louise reappears in my field of vision. She hasn't moved an inch and is still sitting on the edge of the sofa, wearing a dress that should be forbidden.

TWENTY-ONE

She likes Dan, I can tell by Charlotte's red earlobes. Her ears have always given her away.

The champagne in my glass bubbles. I am grateful for the alcohol because without its help, I would have fainted under the Marquis' touch. His eyes speak to me in a language I didn't know he mastered.

As I spot his tall silhouette in the crowd, I breathe a sigh of relief. Something inexplicable about him always gives me a sense of security.

He approaches me. Charlotte sneaks a curious peek at us.

He leans in close to me and whispers in my ear, "You're not drunk, are you? That would be a shame because then I'd have to take care of you."

I definitely need a moment to gather myself. It's all too much at once.

"Excuse me for a moment, I need to use the restroom."

He nods and steps aside to let me pass.

"Charlotte, will you come with me to the bathroom?"

What a question. The brief pause is exactly what we need to catch up with each other.

"Do you like him?" I ask excitedly as we wash our hands side by side.

"He's okay."

"Okay? That doesn't sound very enthusiastic."

"Okay as in - I don't feel sick talking to him and he smells good, but he has an extreme need to brag about his wealth. Did you know he owns twelve sports cars? No? Neither did I - and I could have done without that information."

She applies fresh lipstick. Her reflection grins at me.

"Seriously though, I'm infinitely grateful to you for organizing this meeting. At this point, I would marry absolutely anyone who is willing and can somehow promise to protect me from Gino."

Smiling, I hug her from the side. "You don't owe that to me, but to the Marquis."

"By the way, what's going on between you two?"

I curse my bright red face. "We're married."

"Louise…"

"I don't know what you mean."

"Alright. But I warn you - you've never been able to hide a secret from me."

She pulls me back to our seats. I almost feel like a normal twenty one-year-old woman - and it's wonderful.

But my euphoria comes to an abrupt end when I see the Marquis' face.

That's not him. That's the devil.

He's still beautiful, but the anger in his gaze brings tears to my eyes. A vein throbs on his neck.

That's the Marquis, of whom I've heard whispers.

The Marquis whom I've been warned about. The Marquis who has paid with his soul for his position.

He stands face to face with Dane. His forehead almost touches that of his friend. He grins at him.

One breath.

Two breaths.

Blackout.

My lungs implode.

Dane's nose changes its shape.

The Marquis clenches his hand into a fist, and his muscles twitch dangerously.

He kneels over the helpless man, striking him over and over again until blood soaks through his white shirt.

I have to reach him.

Oh God, oh God, oh God.

"Stop!" My hands slide off his shoulders.

He is as hard as a rock and as destructive as a hurricane.

"Jerome!"

The sound of his name snaps him out of his trance. Dark blonde hair falls in sweaty strands across his face. I have never spoken his name before...

He stares at me with an open mouth, a splatter of blood on his lip.

"You bastard," Dane gurgles.

The Marquis awakens from his ecstasy. He grabs his jacket, seizes my arm, and drags me towards the exit. Charlotte runs after us.

This is how it will always be with him, I think,

stumbling behind him, struggling to keep up: people with fearful eyes stepping back from him, joy turning into panic, an unspoken danger, bitter disappointment in my heart.

And I remember exactly why I never wanted to marry him.

My body is in shock. Violence has been a constant companion since childhood, but I have never grown accustomed to seeing people bleed.

Charlotte slams the car door shut. We wait until she's seated before he hits the gas.

My father is dead.

My husband is a monster.

His fingers grip the steering wheel, his knuckles turning white.

When we stop in front of the castle entrance, I finally look up at him.

"What has gotten into you? What the fuck happened?"

He shakes his head.

"Louise, you're in shock."

Angry, I grab his shoulder. He looks into my eyes and into my soul.

"Tell me right now what happened. Did it have something to do with Charlotte? If so, I need to know."

"It was nothing."

"If *that* is nothing to you, then what happens when you actually get angry?"

His jaw almost jumps out of his face as he clenches

his teeth tightly.

"Talk to me."

He closes his eyes.

"Please!"

His gaze is merciless and deadly.

"Dane approached me while you were in the bathroom and mentioned that your sister was nice, but that he'd rather trade places with me and… take you to his bedroom. To put it politely."

The dark shadows of the night weigh heavily on my heart.

"He said that our marriage was a lie, a transaction, and that it wouldn't hurt me to share you with him. *That's* what happened."

His scent seeps under my skin.

My heart can't keep up with the pace of my thoughts.

"Let's forget about this evening, Louise. It doesn't mean anything."

He gets out of the car and leaves me behind.

TWENTY-TWO

Three days pass and the Marquis is nowhere to be found.

On the fourth day, he sits at the table in the dining hall as I come in for dinner.

I feel so lonely in his realm. Since the incident at the club, I haven't seen my sister. My mother refuses to leave the house.

Where do dreams go when they are forgotten? Do they die silently or do they seek a new owner, someone braver and strong enough to bring them to life?

The Marquis cuts a lobster in half.

"Give me your plate."

"No thank you. I don't eat animals that are cooked alive."

A shadow of a smile flickers across his soft lips. "Why am I not surprised?"

Since I've been living with him, no dish has been repeated. The Marquis' chefs prepare a new creation every evening, each one more refined than the last.

"Where have you been the past few days?"

I make an effort to sound casual. I don't want to give him the impression that I miss him while he's off traveling the world.

"Washington," he replies curtly.

I make a mental note to later search the news feed

for his name to find out what business took him there.

I shouldn't care, but when you spend 24 hours a day alone, there isn't much else to think about.

"Have you heard from Dane again?"

He dabs at the corners of his mouth with his napkin. "Yes. He's devastated about how the evening turned out."

"Could you be more specific?"

"He's devastated that his loose tongue has brought him excommunication, and as the rumors go, he's now back living in his parents' house."

With a questioning look, I set my fork aside.

Women like me are expected to blindly follow the rules of a world whose true face is never revealed to us.

Men like the Marquis guard the secrets that I am so desperate to know.

"What does this mean for him?" I ask.

"An excommunicated man has no friends. No partners to do business with. No clubs that will grant him entry. No woman who will marry him. All he has left is the ticking of time as he watches his wealth slowly dissipate."

Lola enters the room with a new bottle of wine. I'm glad to see her.

"And all of this because he made a joke about wanting to sleep with me?"

He precisely and stoically dissects the lobster.

"No one jokes about what belongs to me."

The lump in my throat steals my appetite.

A furball creeps across the thick carpet towards the Marquis. Effortlessly, it jumps off the floor and lands on his lap.

"Since when do we have a cat?"

I watch in fascination as he starts stroking her fur, hitting all the right spots. The cat relaxes and begins to massage his thigh with its soft paws.

"Since yesterday. I bought her for you on my trip. She'll keep you company whenever you feel lonely."

I swallow hard. He seems to observe me more closely than I thought.

"Thank you," I say.

He feeds our new roommate a piece of lobster. She's already head over heels in love with him.

"I do care about your feelings, Louise, even if it doesn't seem that way. I made a promise to your father, and I will keep it: to make sure you're well taken care of."

The cold tone doesn't match his warm words.

My throat burns.

"The last time I spoke to Albert, I told him that we've never been a real family. That he never loved Mother and didn't love us children either. I hate myself so much for making that the last thing he heard from me."

I can no longer hold back the tears. They fall down my cheeks into my lap.

"He knew you loved him."

"How could you possibly know that?"

"I could see it in his eyes when he walked you down the aisle."

I want to say something.

That I firmly believe that every person can change.

That I know his heart is not dead, but only sleeping deep within.

That power does not hold our hand when we take our last breath one day.

His phone gets ahead of me. The vibration interrupts the silence. He looks at the display, then at me.

"I have to answer this. It's Gino."

TWENTY-THREE
The Marquis

His raspy voice tells of a reckless life without regard for consequences.

"My son," he says, and I know I'm in trouble. "How are you?"

In all the years we've known each other, he's only called me twice.

Once after I killed my father and he wanted to congratulate me.

The second time when he needed my permission to abduct a family.

This third time can't be good. I can tell by how he emphasizes every word too strongly.

"I heard you've sided with the nocturnal creatures," he mocks when I don't respond.

"What do you want from me, old man?"

"An explanation."

Blood rushes in my ears. Gino has had his eyes on my position for far too long. I should have put a stop to him a long time ago.

Louise is just an excuse for him to get closer to me. He wants to overthrow me.

"How come you excommunicate an old school friend?"

My hand grips the phone so tightly that it might shatter any second.

"We had our differences."

"Differences, I see."

Instinctively, I turn around. I've closed the door to the dining hall behind me, but I want to make sure Louise doesn't overhear our conversation, so I start walking towards the mirror hall.

"Dane Gilbertson happened to cross my path today."

Nothing happens by chance in our circles.

"We smoked a cigar together. Had a conversation, as one does, you know. About life and mutual acquaintances."

My chest tightens.

"Is there a point to your story or can I let you ramble on and pretend to listen?"

"I like you, my son."

I am not your son - and my father lies beneath the earth because I put him there.

"Between us, purely hypothetically speaking. Let's say I heard a rumor that you almost bashed Dane Gilbertson's head in because he made a little joke about your fake wife. But from a reliable source, I knew that you feel nothing for said fake wife. After all, you promised to deliver her to me in... less than seven months."

"So, let's say a faint suspicion arose in me, suggesting that you might have developed feelings for the girl, which would then raise the possibility that you won't uphold our agreement. Tell me, my dear Marquis - hypothetically speaking - what would you do if you were in my position?"

There are 83 different types of pistols hanging on the wall of my armory, and each one would fit perfectly to the shape of his head.

I speak through clenched teeth. "I would remind myself that the Marquis is a man of his word. And I would start living each day more intensely, as if it could be my last. Because they say he doesn't respond very kindly to threats."

I end the call.

What a filthy filthy bastard.

TWENTY-FOUR

The Marquis has completely upgraded my wardrobe after our wedding. I only kept my underwear and sleepwear.

My rooms are most beautiful at night, when the moon shines through the tall windows, and the gardens stretch out beneath me.

In the dim light, I sit at the end of the bed and gaze outside. The sight of sleping nature soothes my soul.

After the interruption of the call, the Marquis did not return for dinner. When he disappears, it is always sudden.

There's a knock on the door. Three short and quick knocks. Speak of the devil.

"Come in."

The Marquis enters my bedroom with an air of naturalness, as if we were true spouses. As if he were used to seeing me in my sleepwear.

My shoulders tense up. Since there's an open fire burning in the fireplace, keeping the room warm despite the icy temperatures outside, I'm wearing nothing but a delicate silk negligee. I did not expect his visit.

He stops in the middle of the room.

I wish I had time to admire his beauty in peace. Whenever we spend time together, I force myself to avoid lingering on his noble features, the perfectly curved nose, the regal lips, the green eyes.

He must never think that he could appeal to me.

"I didn't mean to disturb you. I was hoping you were still awake."

"It's only ten o'clock."

He tilts his head slightly back.

"I don't know your sleeping habits, Louise."

"Did you come here just to tell me that?"

It's only now that I notice he's holding something in his hand.

"I came to give you this," he says, extending his hand as he hands me a cellphone.

"Thank you, but I already have one."

I'm aware that the Marquis is stuck in a past century, but does he really assume I don't own a phone?

"From now on, you will only use this one. I will keep your old one," he says, speaking quickly before I can protest. "I honestly should have thought of it earlier. Gino can track you through your current device. This one is equipped with special software that makes it impossible to hack into the system. Wherever you are, he won't be able to find you. Unless he has your number. Which won't happen."

The fireplace casts eerie shadows on his face. "I am the only one who can reach you. When it rings, you'll know it's me," he says, his gaze trailing along my body, over the silk of my nightgown and the contours of my breasts. He lingers a breath too long at the level of my nipples.

A NOBLE CONTRACT

"I swore to protect you and I won't break my word."

TWENTY-FIVE

When the strongest person in your life suddenly loses all their strength, you become aware of the transience of things.

Even when everything seemed hopeless, when I no longer knew what to do and was convinced that there was no solution to my problems - Mother knew what to do.

She was the captain who kept our family's ship on course. The lighthouse that guided us through every storm. Even though she often drove us crazy, she was always the one we could rely on for her steadfastness.

I look at her pale face. This is no longer my mother.

Her hair is unkempt and loose. Dirt clings under her fingernails. Her eyes look tired, staring out the window.

Charlotte said she no longer moves from Father's former study during the day and sometimes even sits there all night.

"Hello, Mother."

She doesn't react to my voice. She is trapped in a distant world.

"I came to ask how you're doing."

Nothing.

"I miss Albert a lot."

Only at the sound of his name does she awaken

from her daydream. She turns her head towards me, and I am startled by how weak she truly looks.

"It's good that you came, Louise. Please have a seat."

The maid has prepared tea for us along with some English pastries. To keep my hands occupied, I dip a cookie into the warm beverage and watch as the dough slowly dissolves.

The ticking of the clock is too loud.

"How are you doing?"

My question doesn't do justice to the feeling that tears you apart when a loved one is gone, I am aware of that. But somehow, I have to fill the silence, or else I'll lose my mind.

"Don't worry about me my child. I knew this day had to come. I was aware that Albert and I would have little time left together. Yet, it still feels like the ground is being ripped from beneath your feet when it actually happens."

"One is never prepared for death," I say as gently as possible. "Even when you know it's on its way."

Mother nods, her face hardening. "How is the Marquis?" She no longer wants to talk about Father.

Gratefully, I go along with the change of topic. "Fine, I suppose. We don't really talk much. Everyone lives their own life and expects nothing from the other."

Translated: *He* lives his life, flying from Paris to Manhattan, then to Sydney and Moscow, and sometimes brings me gifts from his travels. They lie on my bed when I enter my bedroom in the evening, without a note.

He attends important meetings, shakes hands with impressive personalities, while I sit in silent rooms, passing the time, reading about my husband in the newspaper to keep up with where he is at the moment.

Occasionally, I encounter Madison in the hallway, who deliberately ignores me. She still hates me, of course.

"Have you been able to get used to him? I know he's not an easy person. I only met him a few times before your engagement, but I knew him from your father's stories and can imagine that he doesn't make it easy for you."

Wow. This has to be the most honest conversation I've ever had with my mother.

"Honestly, he ignores me most of the day, if he's even home at all."

Home. That word still sounds so wrong.

"Perhaps that's actually the best thing that could have happened to you," she says, scratching her chin. "Definitely better than floating in his lake with a gunshot wound to the head."

I try to find any signs on her face that she's attempting a joke, but her expression remains serious.

"What's the worst thing the Marquis has ever done?" I ask, my throat dry.

"We don't talk about that, Louise." My name sounds sharp on her tongue. That's the mother I know.

"I'm an adult. I can handle bitter truths. Especially since I'm used to people who would kill for their own gain. I grew up with them."

She doesn't respond to my dig. Instead, she gestures towards the teapot.

"Very well. As you wish. Would you please pour me another cup?"

Steam scented with blossoms and cloves rises from our cups as I refill them.

Mother and I don't share many similarities, but we both prefer our tea without sugar. We both prefer things raw. Pure. Just as they truly are.

She takes a sip from her cup, and I watch as with each passing minute, she regains more of her old demeanor.

It's good for her to think about things that have nothing to do with my father.

"But remember, you will spend your life with him. Sometimes, it's wiser to overlook the secrets of the people closest to us."

"As I said, I am an adult."

Her finger traces along the her cup. "We never told you much about his background for a good reason. We wanted you to get to know him without any prejudices. Of course, it was inevitable that you would hear stories about him before the wedding, but we did our best."

"The Colberts, as you know, are one of the oldest families in France. For generations, they have managed to maintain their wealth and influence. Even the French Revolution couldn't touch them."

"They owe this success to a trait that runs through all generations: the family consists of strong men. Men who don't care who they hurt or whoever perishes because of them. Men who never lose sight of their goal and don't give up until they possess what they desire."

It's fascinating how differently my mother and I define strength, but now that I finally have her at a point where she openly tells me about the Marquis' past, I don't want to interrupt her.

"The Marquis' father was a tyrant. He kept real people dressed in dog costumes as pets and forced them to live on all fours."

I feel sick.

"I'll spare you the details, but there was a reason he held the position of Chairman of the Circle for over thirty years. No one had ever held that position for as long as he did. He knew how to assert himself – and it was always clear that your husband would eventually take on his role."

I vaguely remember seeing his father's face in one of the many paintings in the former throne room.

Most of the time, I look down when passing by all those spirits captured in oil, because their cold gaze reminds me too much of the Marquis' and it fills me with fear.

"But he was dissatisfied with his son's character. Your husband was weak. He spent too much time with his horses and not enough time hunting. His father noticed early on that he hesitated before pulling the trigger when they were shooting at deers and foxes. He didn't like that. So, he put him to the test."

As I think about how people who don't know our world long for wealth and nobility, I almost burst out laughing. From the outside, everything looks so glamorous, carefree, and aesthetic.

In reality, we are all just chess pieces, and in the end, everyone falls, even the king.

"The Marquis was twenty when his father took him to a Circle meeting. At that time, new board elections were imminent and he had it in his mind to demonstrate to them that his son was strong enough to lead them, despite his young age."

Whatever is about to follow will give me nightmares. But there is no going back.

"And so, in the presence of the twelve most powerful men in the world, he put a gun in his hand. Should I go on?"

She can see how pale I've turned.

My hands are ice-cold.

"Go on."

"I'm almost done anyway. So, he handed him the weapon, tapped his forehead, and said, *If you're a man, then shoot.*"

"And he refused?"

"He proved to be a man."

The Marquis shot his own father… He ended a life

in exchange for power.

I feel sick.

"Does that come as a surprise to you?" Mother's talent for empathy is unique.

"I knew he was a killer." But a hidden part of me secretly hoped that he had only ever killed in self-defense.

Mother sees through me. I can tell she's reading my thoughts, and I'm infinitely grateful when she doesn't press further.

"You know, Louise, I didn't want to marry your father at first either. Our marriage was arranged. My heart belonged to another, but what choice did I have? Over the years, I learned to love your father. Now that he's gone, I am only half. What I'm trying to say is - give him time. Give yourself time. The men of our world are tough, but they would give everything for those they love. I believe that you can find happiness. One day."

This *one day* hides behind forced conversations, stiff touches, and cold glances.

This *one day* will forever be on the run.

If there's one thing I'm sure of, it's that the Marquis and I can never love each other.

To not disappoint her, I still thank Mother for her well-intentioned words and then greet her with a kiss on the cheek.

I need to talk to Charlotte.

My sister is practicing the piano. She doesn't play

as masterfully as the Marquis, but she's on her way there. When she pauses briefly between two songs, I tap her from behind.

"Do you have a moment for me?"

I startle as her dismissive expression catches me off guard.

She simply nods and follows me into the room that used to be mine and now serves as a parlor.

Embarrassed, I sit across from her.

She speaks first. "What do you want?"

I don't understand her anger.

We haven't seen each other since the incident with Dane Gilbertson, but I had assumed she would have processed it well.

"To talk to you. To ask you how you're doing?"

"What do you think, how I'm doing?"

Her fingernails are chewed, her eyes surrounded by dark circles.

Everyone in this house is slowly falling apart.

"Can you slow down a bit? I can't keep up with your mood swings…"

She rolls her eyes. "Of course not. Why would you? Your life isn't at stake. You're all safe."

Her words hurt me deeply. "You know very well that I'm doing everything I can to help you. Why are you suddenly like this?"

Her eyes narrow. "Because *your* husband ruined my chances of a possible rescue."

It's slowly dawning on me. "You can't be serious. He was the one who organized the meeting with

Dane in the first place."

"Only to then break his nose. What a wonderful help."

My face burns hot with anger.

Yes, the Marquis didn't act correctly, but up to the point of the confrontation, he tried to help Charlotte.

"Are you really trying to tell me that you're willing to marry a man who boasts about what he would do with me in the bedroom behind your back?"

This is the last straw for her.

Her blue eyes turn black.

"We all get it," she yells at me and jumps off the couch. "Everyone wants you. You don't have to rub it in my face."

I feel sick. "Damn it, that's not the point at all."

"What is it then? The Marquis wanted to marry *you* and save *your* life. And as if that wasn't enough, he scares off the only man who was willing to get to know me."

I have an angry response burning on the tip of my tongue when I realize what she just said. "What do you mean, he wanted to marry me? For him, this marriage was just as involuntary as it was for me. Our parents practically forced him into it."

She snorts. "Do you seriously still believe that?"

My vision goes black.

"He approached Albert. He knew the danger our entire family was in, and he offered to marry one of us. You, to be precise."

"How do you know?"

"Mother told me yesterday."

"And why did they keep that hidden from me? Why did they let me believe it was about some old debt?"

"It *is* about debt. It's true that the Marquis owed our family a favor. But they didn't even think about blackmailing him. They would never have considered asking the head of the Circle for something so big."

"I don't understand anything anymore."

"He saw you at the debutante ball. Don't you remember he was there?"

"No."

I went with Gabriel as my kavalier, my school friend, whom I haven't seen since I got married.

"He saw you and approached our parents the same evening to make his proposal. He marries you, in turn they erase his debt. Of course, they agreed immediately."

This changes everything.

Above all, it takes away any trust I had.

I believed my parents.

I believed the Marquis, as foolish as it must sound.

They deceived me.

"But why?"

"What do I know? Maybe he likes virgins and wants to fuck you? Ask me something better."

She is still so combative that it makes no sense to continue the conversation.

I reach for my jacket.

"Anyway. Even if that's the case - it wasn't my

decision to be saved. I would have gladly fought this battle without the support of a power-hungry, ruthless man. Get some proper sleep, then we'll talk again."

The circles under her eyes look unhealthy.

She doesn't pay attention to my words.

Silently, I leave the house that once used to be my home and that now makes me feel like a stranger.

TWENTY-SIX

When the Marquis isn't traveling to foreign lands, he spends most of his time at opulent balls.

I've been attending events of this kind since I was a child, but the number of invitations piling up on his desk is unmatched.

On my bed lies a dress made of golden silk, along with matching jewelry, the value of which I'd rather not know.

It's a gift from the Marquis.

As I make my way down the stairs two hours later, all dressed up, he's waiting for me in the entrance hall, dressed in a tailcoat.

I have to cling to the railing with every step to keep from falling forward.

Whenever he looks at me, it feels as if I could confide every one of my secrets to him and he would not judge me for anything, but rather securely hold each feeling.

It's foolish of me to think like that.

His beautiful exterior conceals the darkness within him.

I lay awake all night because I couldn't get the image of the twenty-year-old Marquis, who shot his father, out of my head.

Thank goodness for make up.

"You look beautiful. The dress is made for you."

He's right. My dark hair forms the perfect contrast to the golden shimmering fabric, and the cut flatters my curves so gracefully that I feel like a Greek goddess.

When I place my hand in his, the touch feels right.

He knew me.

He offered to marry me.

I would love nothing more than to ask him about my sister's words, but I have to find the perfect moment for it.

If you catch the Marquis off guard, he shuts down and all answers are lost forever.

Together we drive to the old opera house, where the ball is taking place tonight.

I can hardly breathe, I'm so excited. It's the first time I'm attending a public event without Charlotte by my side. I don't know anyone there. I will be completely reliant on the Marquis.

He helps me out of the carriage. Immediately, all eyes are on us. The list of women who have fought for his love is endless. Each of them would kill to be in my place right now.

"Ready?" he whispers in my ear.

"No."

"Then let's get it over with."

He places his hand on my lower back. I shiver under his touch. A tingling sensation travels from his hand to between my thighs.

He pushes me into the crowd. The diamonds

around my neck sparkle. For the first time in a long while, I feel truly beautiful.

For the Marquis, the ball is nothing more than an obligation. Every two meters, we stop, shake hands, and smile so forced that after the first hour, all my facial muscles are frozen.

"Ten minutes longer with this man and I would have turned into stone," the Marquis whispers in my ear as he pulls me onto the dance floor and we flee from the British ambassador.

We have never danced together before. Not even at our wedding. I must admit that he's an exceptional dancer.

Most men lead hesitantly, with restraint, easily distracted, throwing one off balance. The Marquis, on the other hand, directs every movement with a determination as if the musicians were playing for us alone.

His gaze is fixed firmly on me. We spin round and round in circles, flying past other couples, never once losing our balance.

"You dance well," he smirks down at me.

"Coming from you, that means a lot."

I shouldn't flatter his ego any further, but tonight my thoughts seem to slip too easily from my lips.

It must be the champagne that the waiters practically throw at you.

"How do you like life by my side so far?"

Does it just seem to me, or has he long been mentally preparing himself to ask me this question?

" It could be worse, but it could also be better."

"What exactly could be better?".

"I often feel very alone"

His green eyes widen in surprise. "And that's a bad thing?"

I laugh. "Loneliness has never really been on my bucket list."

"I enjoy being alone. I don't see the point in spending time with people who don't help me grow."

His words hit me like a punch to the gut.

My face turns red.

He bites his lip. "I'm not talking about you. Your company could be worse."

I have to force myself to suppress a smile. "Can I ask you something?"

"Go ahead. The longer you keep me away from all these idiots waiting to discuss business with me on a night like this, the better."

"My sister mentioned something about you."

His gaze almost indifferently wanders from me to the champagne-sipping and hand-shaking crowd surrounding us.

"She mentioned that you've suggested to my parents to take me as your wife?"

He swallows. For two seconds, he falls out of character, but the mask he has worn for a lifetime is too perfectly tailored to him for him to completely lose it.

His cold gaze meets my expectant one. "And if that were the case?"

"Then I'd be very interested to know why you act as if I'm a burden that was imposed on you, when the marriage was of your own free will?"

I can't read him.

His muscles tense under my touch. "I don't know, Louise."

Men like him always have an answer. They don't show weakness by admitting they are at a loss.

"It's true. I saw you and something inside me persuaded me to help you. I did it without ulterior motives. It was a gut feeling. Nothing more, nothing less."

My fingers dig into his shoulders. If I hurt him, he doesn't show it.

"It's not because... you find me attractive?"

He wrinkles his nose, with all the arrogance that I'm used to from him.

"Don't be ridiculous, Louise. You're a child."

I plummet thirty stories down onto the hard asphalt of reality.

"Louise? Is that you?"

A voice shatters the bubble that has formed around us during the waltz.

I release my grip from the Marquis's shoulders and turn around.

"Gabriel!"

Our paths haven't crossed since I moved away from my hometown.

Euphorically, I throw my arms around him.

Gabriel has been one of my best friends for as long

as I can remember. As children we taught each other how to swim, played hide and seek in his grandparents' castle and imagined how life would unfold for us in the future.

After my engagement, my mother no longer deemed it appropriate for me to meet with him, even though our relationship had always been purely platonic.

And since he understands how the game is played, he accepted it without any resentment.

Seeing him here now, among all these unfamiliar, unwelcoming faces, soothes my soul.

His familiar scent takes me back to distant worlds where I once was carefree.

"What are you doing here?" I ask.

"My parents forced me to accompany them; had I known you would be here, I wouldn't have made such a fuss."

He laughs his genuine laugh. Gabriel has the energy of a Golden Retriever. It's simply impossible not to like him.

Someone clears their throat behind me. Oh shit, in my euphoria, I completely forgot about the Marquis.

As I turn to him, I freeze inside. He glares at Gabriel with such a hateful look that it makes me feel sick.

"Gabriel, this is my husband, the Marquis de Colbert," I try to save the situation.

"A pleasure," Gabriel smiles and extends his hand to my husband.

The latter only reluctantly returns the gesture and says nothing.

"We've known each other since I can remember," I try to explain. "Gabriel has witnessed every embarrassing phase of my life and if he ever utters a word about it... unfortunately, I will be compelled to kill him."

"Fascinating."

Why does the Marquis find it so incredibly easy to make conversations uncomfortable with just one word? Why can't he make a bit of an effort?

He annoys me. His perfectly tailored tuxedo and tightly slicked back hair go perfectly with the stick up his ass.

"Well, my husband seems to be used to more exciting company. Let's not bore him. Do you feel like getting some food and telling me everything that's been happening with you lately?"

Gabriel nods. Without giving the Marquis another glance, I start to make my way towards the buffet when five fingers grip my upper arm and stop me from walking.

"I don't think so," his deep voice growls in my ear. "I think you're tired and just want to go home."

Gabriel looks at us with a raised eyebrow.

I take a deep breath. "And I think an adult woman is perfectly capable of deciding when she needs to be put to bed."

An angry smirk crosses his mouth.

He comes close to my face.

"You have two options. Either you start moving those pretty legs of yours and accompany me home, or I have to figure out how rough you really like it, throw you over my shoulder, and carry you to your bedroom. What do you choose, little one?"

My mouth hangs open.

His words find their way under my skin and to my nipples, which stiffen under the golden fabric.

He sees it.

His gaze moves to my breasts.

"I thought so."

I let myself be pulled through the crowd towards the exit without protest, and I don't even manage to say goodbye to Gabriel.

TWENTY-SEVEN

The tension in the car is unbearable. The air is electrically charged. The Marquis' hand rests on my thigh.

I'm as wet as I've never been before in my life. There's no point in lying to myself any longer.

I want him.

In all positions, in all his majestic size.

What would happen if I were to sleep with him just once? What do I have to lose anyway?

We don't speak a word throughout the entire journey. There is something threatening about the Marquis' silence, as if it could mean everything and nothing at the same time.

He looked jealous when Gabriel stood before us, as if he wanted to do to him what he did to Dane and ruin his handsome face.

But it doesn't add up. I know with absolute certainty that I mean nothing to him. His disinterested gaze reveals it when we sit across from each other at dinner a few times a month.

Since I've been living with him, we haven't had a single conversation that lasted longer than ten minutes.

He can't be jealous.

It's likely about respect. What belongs to him should not be touched in public. No one flirts with the Marquis' wife without facing the consequences, even if that was definitely not Gabriel's intention.

He is gay, but the Marquis doesn't need to know that.

I enjoy this game.

Silently, I follow him out of the car and up the impressive staircase to the castle entrance.

Rousel is still awake and opens the door for us.

A fire is burning in the fireplace. The Marquis turns to me, and his poison spreads through my body.

He opens his mouth to say something, but a shadow enters the room.

"Jerome, there you are," Madison says.

She is always flawless. No matter what time of day or night you encounter her, her hair is perfectly styled, her cheeks covered in just the right amount of blush, and her toned body takes your breath away.

"I've missed you."

They say that the Marquis loves her. But his mouth remains stern as he responds, "Could you give us a moment? I want to speak with Louise."

Despite our only interactions consisting of her trying to make it clear how far I am from playing in her league, I feel compassion for her.

It must feel terrible to love a man, be certain that you will marry him, only to be replaced by a younger woman and silently accept that he presents her to the public as his number one.

Shyly, I smile at her.

"If you're not careful, I'll wipe that smug grin off your face," she hisses at me.

My smile freezes.

"Madison."

The Marquis emphasizes her name in a way that makes my blood run cold. She hears it too. There are battles that cannot be won.

Shrugging, she turns on her heel and leaves us alone.

"I'll be waiting for you in the bedroom."

The Marquis grabs my wrist and pulls me behind him into a more secluded room. It's dark here, with only the millions of individual crystals on the chandeliers sparkling in the moonlight.

He closes the door behind us.

"What do you intend to do?" My voice trembles.

"To warn you."

I always thought I was well-prepared for the world that awaited me outside of my parents' home, but I was wrong.

I am far too soft and easily breakable.

The Marquis stands at a towering two meters, intimidating in his perfectly tailored suit and with a gaze from another era.

Instinctively, I take a step back.

He takes a step forward.

We repeat this dance until I find myself with my back against the wall and him standing close to me.

He looks down at me.

Gino has given me nightmares, but slowly it

dawns on me that I have feared the wrong man.

The devil hides behind false beauty.

The Marquis grabs my chin, his thumb tracing the skin beneath my lower lip.

A dark blonde strand of hair falls onto his face.

"If you ever dare to let another man touch you again, I'm afraid I'll have to kill him."

The temperature drops rapidly.

Goosebumps spread across my bare arms.

The Marquis releases his hand from my chin and starts playing with the fabric of my dress.

"Do you understand, Louise?"

When I don't answer, shock stuck in my throat, he gently places his thumb on my lower lip.

"Can you show me that you're a good girl and do as I say?"

I nod.

He pushes his thumb deeper into my mouth and briefly plays with the tip of my tongue.

"I knew I could count on you."

He releases his spell and steps away from me.

His footsteps carry him into the night, away from me and into the arms of the woman who hates me.

What am I to him? All of this is slowly but surely beginning to grow beyond the limits of a fake marriage.

TWENTY-EIGHT

If there's one thing in the world that the Marquis loves more than money or power, it's his horses.

As a child, I used to compete in riding tournaments, but that was long ago, and after a painful fall on my tailbone, I never dared to get on the back of a horse again.

However, I still love the scent of straw, the loud breathing of these majestic creatures, and the sound of hooves scraping against old stone.

The Marquis' stable is my little paradise.

The only thing that unsettles me is the attached arena where my husband pays female acrobats to ride his horses and give him private performances whenever he desires.

The message is clear: Women are beautiful objects to him, to be admired, but never to raise their voices or express their own opinions. His soul is stuck in the 18th century.

Ombre is my favorite horse. His spirit is calmer than the others, which is why the Marquis never rides him - he doesn't find pleasure in passive beings lacking fighting spirit.

He's a man addicted to competition and only respects beings that reflect himself. That's why he ignores Ombre.

I, on the other hand, love him. His soft hair shines

under my hand as I gently groom him.

It has become our little tradition for me to visit the stable every morning before eight and spend time with him.

At first, he was shy. His branding mark is poorly healed, and I sense that he doesn't trust humans, but over time, he has grown accustomed to me.

Lost in thought, I hum a soft melody.

I am deeply absorbed in the meditative movements, so I don't hear his footsteps. It's only when the Marquis stops next to me and clears his throat that I notice him.

I shrink back. Ombre flinches as well. I place a calming hand on his back before he starts to panic.

"What are you doing here?"

No *"Good morning,"* no *"How are you?"* Straight to the point.

I've never seen him in anything other than one of his unique suits. Today, he's wearing a dark gray, slightly sparkling variation consisting of three pieces. The Albert chain with a golden pocket watch is attached to it as always. Without this accessory, which seems more fitting for the 1920s than our modern times, and the brooch with his family crest on his chest, the Marquis never leaves the house.

His wardrobe expresses how strongly he holds onto the values of old nobility.

He notices my scrutiny.

"Do you like what you see?" he asks in a deep voice, and I blush.

"I was thinking of something else," I try to talk my way out of it.

"Whatever, that doesn't answer my original question. What are you doing here? My men have informed me that you spend your mornings in my stables and... clean out? Are you aware that there is staff for that?" He has both arms on his hips and is tapping his foot.

"I enjoy doing it. It takes my mind off things and it's good for me to move. Otherwise, I'll lose my mind."

As Ombre approaches the Marquis with his wet nose, he moves back a few inches to keep his suit from getting dirty.

"You know we have a gym? And a swimming pool? If you want, I can hire a personal trainer for you. You don't have to clean out stables if you're looking for physical activity; there are plenty of other options here..."

His mouth twitches. I blush. No, he didn't mean it in a suggestive way. That wouldn't be like him.

"But I want to spend time with the horses," I say as my hand runs along Ombre's neck. He snorts. "They're good for me."

The Marquis raises an eyebrow in surprise. "I didn't know you shared my love for racehorses."

"They don't have to be racehorses. I don't care about their performance. I love their soul."

"Their soul..." A malicious smirk tugs at his mouth. "Can you ride?"

My pride overwhelms me from behind. "Of course," I reply more brusquely than intended. "I competed in tournaments for seven years."

"And why did you stop?"

My throat suddenly goes dry. I clear it. "Out of fear."

"Fear..." he repeats thoughtfully. The words on his lips sounds as if he's searching for its meaning, as if he doesn't know what feeling I'm talking about because he's never experienced it himself. "Fear of what?"

I could tell him that it was the fear of falling off a horse again and waking up in the hospital with a broken leg, but that would be a lie. So I choose the truth.

"I was good at show jumping. Very good, in fact. My trainer predicted a successful career for me. But something deep inside me was holding me back. The fact that everyone around me believed in me so strongly made it even harder. Because I knew all eyes were on me. If I had failed, everyone would have seen it. So, I gave up what I did best out of fear of failing."

With each sentence, I close myself off a little more to protect myself from his reaction. I'm almost certain he will laugh at me, but his face remains serious.

"I understand," he says instead, and before I know it, he has suddenly grabbed my hips and I'm flying through the air. Effortlessly, he lifts my full body weight, swings me forward, and sets me on Ombre's back.

The horse remains calm, not resisting me.

"What is this?" I protest, filled with fear, my fingers clutching the mane. I want to jump off, but the Marquis still has one hand on my hip, the other resting on my thigh.

He looks me directly in the eyes. "You only get rid of fear by showing it that you're not afraid of it." My muscles tense up. "Nothing can happen to you, Louise. I'm with you."

So high above the ground, I have difficulty breathing, but the certainty that the Marquis will catch me if I fall gradually calms my heartbeat. Still, my hands are cold and sweaty.

"How does it feel?"

"Terrifying."

If someone had told me a few weeks ago that I would be back on the back of a horse today, I would have called them crazy. Yet here I am, brave and strong. Two character traits that I rarely attribute to myself.

The Marquis takes a step back from me. My shoulders tense up again. When I see what he intends to do, I open my eyes in shock. "Don't you dare."

"Easy there, little one," he winks at me and does the unthinkable: he opens the gate, gives Ombre a decisive pat on the flank, and calmly watches as the horse carries me past him out of the stable.

Everything inside me screams, but I know I have to stay calm to avoid making Ombre nervous, because that could end badly. The Marquis has put me in a more than dangerous situation. Ombre is not saddled, I have no reins to hold onto if necessary. If he starts running, I will fall.

Fortunately, he walks leisurely towards the paddock. The Marquis effortlessly keeps pace thanks to his long legs.

He has outsmarted me. Again. I made him aware of the effort it takes for me to trust a horse. To be reminded of my shattered dreams. He knows I have to force myself to remain calm and control my emotions if I don't want to get hurt. This is one of his sick lectures.

As Ombre sets his hooves on soft grass, I feel better. Deeply relaxed, he starts grazing and snorts contentedly.

I glare angrily at my husband.

"Get me down immidiately."

"At your command."

He grabs me, and just as quickly as I was up there, I am now back down. He looks down at me.

"Asshole," I hiss. I entrusted him with my most intimate weakness, and he made a game out of it.

Determined, I walk away across the paddock, heading back towards the stables. He follows me without saying a word. I can feel his presence on my neck.

"Louise."

"Leave me alone."

"Louise!" The Marquis grabs my arm, whirls me

around, and hurls me against the nearest wall. His jaw clenches. His eyes darken with anger.

"Let go of me!"

His breath tickles my face. "You have no right to be angry right now."

"That's interesting coming from Monsieur Self-Control. You've already demonstrated how well you keep your cool when you're angry," I allude to the incident with Dane Gilbertson at the club.

His nostrils flare as he exhales deeply. "I just wanted to help you overcome your fear."

"That's what you call helping? I knew you were an ice block, but…"

Before I can say another word, he pulls the ground away from under me and does the one thing I never, not in this universe or any parallel one, would have thought possible: he kisses me.

I can't breathe. I'm drowning. In him. His fingers dig into my open hair as his lower body presses me forcefully against the wall. I feel his arousal. His lips touch mine as if they always belonged there, as if my mouth were the home he's been searching for.

I can't help it. I return the kiss. I part my lips to grant him entry. He immediately follows the invitation. Our tongues meet, circle each other, play with each other.

I feel him in every corner of my body. A moan escapes my chest. It snaps him out of his trance. Shocked by himself, with widened eyes and flushed lips, he backs away from me. Shyly, I tuck a strand of hair behind my ear that he's tousled.

"That was a mistake," he blurts out.

I blush even more. Shame pours over me and clogs my lungs.

I am a mistake. I always have been one.

He starts walking backward, moving away from me, then turns around. With quick steps, he flees from me without giving me another glance. His broad shoulders disappear from my view.

Ground, swallow me up. I'm ready to burn in hell.

TWENTY-NINE
The Marquis

Under my bed, there's always a packed suitcase waiting. My private plane is always fully fueled, and a pilot is on standby at all times.

When I'm on the run, I feel closest to myself. I love burning bridges behind me. It keeps me alive.

The plane starts moving. Taking a deep breath, I lean back, sinking deeper into the buttery soft leather of the seat. When that doesn't relax my muscles, I press a button to activate the massage function.

Straining, I close my eyes, but immediately open them again when all I see in front of me are her innocent eyes and the swollen lips that would look so wonderful around my dick.

I must disappear for as long as possible. She is thin ice, and beneath her surface, my certain death is waiting for me. I know that she will be my end, but I am trying to avoid this inevitable fate for as long as I still have the strength to do so.

"May I get you something to drink, Monsieur?" The stewardess is wearing a skirt that is too short and a skin-tight blouse. I have to use all my mental strength to stop myself from bending her over one of the seats and ramming my cock between her legs from behind to stop thinking about Louise for at least a few minutes.

"Whiskey on ice."

She nods and walks down the hallway. I look at her ass. Louise's ass is small and firm. *Keep it together.*

Even if Gino hadn't woken me up at five this morning to inform me that he wants to convene the Circle for an unscheduled meeting, I would have left France.

I don't know what got into me. I should never have kissed Louise. That boundary should never have been crossed.

Gino can only convene a Circle meeting with my permission. I allowed it because I'm curious about what is so important that twelve men from all continents of the world have to travel and set aside their commitments within a day.

It can't mean anything good.

A year will pass quickly. I promised him my wife's life. There is no turning back.

There is only one reason why this body, which I know to be nothing but rock-hard and unshakable, lost control yesterday. It's her damned gaze when she looks at me, as if I could protect her, as if I *would* protect her, and as if my personality is just a charade behind which lies a good heart.

She said it - that she believes I'm not the bad person everyone thinks I am.

She's wrong.

Gino is already waiting for me at the airport. I had a car pick me up, but I didn't expect him to be sitting in the back seat. I don't like that. In the back of my mind, I make a note to find out who was responsible for arranging the transport. Another life to ruin. The list is slowly becoming worryingly long.

I sit down next to the old Italian on the leather bench. He's smoking a cigar. If the car weren't rented but one of my private ones, I would chop off his hand right then and there.

"What do you want?" I ask gruffly, instead of a formal greeting. I don't even look at him; instead, I stare hard out the window. Chicago flies past us.

"Is that how you speak to old friends?"

"I have no friends."

My head is about to explode. Since we started our descent, I can't think straight anymore. It hurts not to be on the same continent as Louise. I'm sick.

"You disappointed me, Jerome."

"Call me by my first name again and I'll make your Sicilian ancestors proud." I slowly turn my head and look into his eyes. "Tell me Gino. Do you prefer acid or hungry pigs?"

He swallows. I like it when people are afraid of me. I feed on fear. When I feel something breaking because of me, my soul blossoms.

"I have come to prepare you for what I will address later in the meeting. Because I care about you, my son, and hoped that we would do business together in the future. But it seems you prefer to fight alone."

"That's the first thing I've heard from you that

doesn't make me doubt your sanity."

He takes a drag on his cigar. "Don't overestimate yourself, Jerome. Everyone loses at some point. And it's always those we least expect who bring us down."

We pull up in front of the tallest skyscraper in the city. Jet lag is weighing heavy on my bones. I've skipped almost an entire day.

Night falls upon us as Gino and I simultaneously slam the car doors shut behind us.

Side by side, we march through the glass revolving door, into the elevator, and silently ascend towards the sky. We both know that there's no place reserved for us up there. Hell was created for men like us.

Gino lets me step out of the elevator first, because he's smart and wants to keep his tongue.

When my father forced me to shoot him, he gave me the best gift a father can leave behind. He killed every ounce of compassion in me.

All eleven men are already seated side by side at the long table. Gino joins them as the twelfth. I take my place in the honorary chair designated for me.

"Gentlemen, as you know, Gino di Lanza has requested a special meeting, and I have approved it. He will now present his concerns to you. We have sixty minutes."

With that, I reach for the hourglass on the table in front of me and turn it upside down. The sand begins to trickle slowly. The visible dying of time reminds me that Louise's end is inevitably drawing closer.

I clear my throat and adjust my tie. It's tied too tightly. I can't breathe.

Gino rises from his chair. His hands are clasped behind his back. He's a dishonest man.

"Gentlemen, thank you for your last minute attendance. I appreciate it," he says, running a hand through his thin hair. "As you may know, I had a small business dispute with the head of the de Guise family."

The name sends shivers down my arms. Albert's chair isn't empty. His place has already been taken by a man who is richer and wiser than he was.

I wonder at what point Louise's father began to let his emotions guide him and lose control of his actions. Was he aware of what he was doing when he made Gino his enemy, or was he so blinded by emotions that he only realized his mistake when it was too late? I wonder if his fate could befall any of us.

My phone lights up. It can't be Louise. When I travel, I always leave my private phone behind. She has no way to reach me, and all the doors that could grant her access to my thoughts are locked.

You're already thinking about her constantly. Gino's voice snaps me out of my thoughts.

"Marquis."

I look up at him.

"We all know that you're the most competent leader who could rule over the Circle. You do it with an iron hand and never waver from your decisions. This strength of will protects us and our secrets," Gino says.

My jaw twitches. I can't quite grasp what he's getting at, and I don't like it one bit.

"Time is running out. Please get to the point," I say, giving a stern look at the hourglass.

"Of course. Marquis, you are familiar with the old traditions. I don't need to explain to you what it means when I ask for a blood oath from you?"

I almost choke on my own spit. Fortunately, I excel at putting on a poker face, so Gino doesn't realize he's hit a nerve.

He's doing this because he wants my position. It's no longer about Louise for him. He must have discovered something in my eyes when we talked about her that he's now using against me.

He understood that she meant something to me before I could even realize it myself, and if my naivety is going to be my downfall, then damn it, I deserve it.

None of this should have ever happened.

"Some of the members present here are new. Not all of those gathered here today have witnessed a blood oath, which is why I will explain my reasons once again," Gino says. He seems so self-assured, so convinced of himself and his black soul that I want to torture him and see him choke on his own blood.

"The Marquis," - his sausage-like fingers point at me - "has given me a promise. We all know that he married Louise de Guise only to protect her from my revenge. But we also know that no one who tries to deceive me should expect too much from life." His gaze drills into mine too intensely.

"Louise de Guise must die. Her father has betrayed me. Deceiving a brother of the Circle brings death upon oneself and one's family. I am a suspicious man. Even though I know that nothing in this world means more to you, Monsieur le Marquis, than your honor, I still want your promise in blood. The promise that I can kill Louise after a year has passed since your marriage."

He's right. Our brotherhood is one of the oldest, it has survived for centuries, enduring wars and revolutions, only because we follow the rules. Without a framework that gives us stability while preventing us from breaking out, we would all be just ordinary men.

But we are rulers. Rulers are not governed by emotions. They rule those who are weak enough to follow their hearts.

My head nods of its own accord. "If you demand my blood, Gino, I will give it to you. And I swear with my life to sacrifice Louise de Guise in your honor."

I reach into the inside of my jacket and grab the slim golden knife that resides at my heart and accompanies me everywhere I go. Another quick hand movement and my thumb starts bleeding.

Gino does the same. A cut into flesh, a step

towards me. We press our fingertips together and look into each other's eyes.

"I swear," I say in a hoarse voice. "I swear that I will deliver Louise de Guise if you demand it. Should external motives prevent me from fulfilling this promise, I will sacrifice my own life in her place."

A small voice whispers to me that I deserve to pay for my sins with my life.

THIRTY
The Marquis

I take a deep breath and choke on the smoke of my cigar. Cuban cigars are usually my favorite, but today they taste of loneliness.

In my penthouse in Chicago, I have always felt safe, so high above the ground, with the city lights lying at my feet and a security system that the English king could learn from.

But tonight, I am restless. The shadows in my bedroom lay on my shoulders, on my soul, and breathe their black breath into me.

I sit in a leather chair and gaze out at Chicago. I am afraid. Not of my enemies. Not of Louise. But of myself.

My phone vibrates. An Italian name lights up on the display, a name I had intended to forget for the evening.

"Gino. I thought everything was said after our meeting today?"

"I wanted to speak with you privately once more, but you were out the door and gone in an instant."

"I had important obligations." Standing under the shower, staring at the marble for over an hour, while all the water in the world fails to wash away my sins.

"Anyway. We can talk over the phone. I have something to tell you, Jerome."

I despise that he calls me by my first name, but at least he only does it in private. If it were to happen during a meeting, I couldn't guarantee anything.

"I don't want to have you as an enemy," he says, pressing his mouth too tightly against the phone, so that I can almost feel his wet breath in my ear.

"Demanding a blood oath from someone clearly shows that you do not trust their word. You have demonstrated to the Circle that my word is not enough for you. If that doesn't sound like a declaration of war, my dear Gino, then what is it?"

He clears his throat. *Good. Make him nervous.*

"A wake-up call. You are losing yourself, Jerome, I can see it in your eyes."

"Choose your words wisely now."

"Don't worry. I don't intend to offend you. But you know that your father and I were close friends, and after his death, I made it my mission to keep a watchful eye on you."

"No one asked you to do that."

He ignores my objection. "So far, you have done impressively well. You have never missed a single meeting. You are always well-prepared and know which men to befriend and which ones to keep at a distance. I have always been proud of you."

I notice how he's speaking in the past tense. "After you brutally attacked Dane Gilbertson in public, I knew something was wrong. A man of your class doesn't do such things. We choose different paths, more discreet ones. We don't cause scandals."

"I would like to disagree with you, but unfortunately, you have a point there."

"I know, Jerome, I know. You've lost control."

It was one damn evening. A single, life-changing evening. I should never have let my hand slip. From a young age, I was trained to kill emotions at the root. Losing control means losing power.

"When I found out that you publicly fought over a girl, I knew something was wrong. That's why I made you swear. Because I'm not sure anymore that you trust your own promises to yourself."

"I gave you my word. Nothing ties me to Louise de Guise. When she's gone, my life will go back to how it was before. That suits me just fine. Madison is getting worried."

"Are you sure about that, Jerome? That everything will be as it was before? Can you look me in the eye and promise that you won't intervene at the last minute to save her?"

A colorful mix of countless images rushes past my mind's eye. The golden fabric of her dress. The shiny hair of a black horse. The beige tulle of her wedding veil. Her father's red blood on her mother's hands. The hope in her blue eyes when she looked at me.

No one has ever trusted me. People did business with me because I have influence, and they entrusted me with tasks because I am strong and cold. But never has anyone looked at me and trusted that I wouldn't disappoint them. And then came Louise.

But Gino is right. Emotions are unreliable.

Emotions don't vote for you when you have a position to defend, they don't protect you from gunshot wounds, and they don't give any power that would be useful to me.

"You can trust me, Gino. She belongs to you."

"Good. You will understand that the women of the de Guise family are cunning creatures, beautiful liars who will blind you with their false truths and make you oblivious to what really happens. Don't be misled, Marquis. It's not too late yet."

THIRTY-ONE

For a month, I haven't heard from the Marquis. He doesn't call. He doesn't write. He doesn't visit.

For two months, I've been walking alone in the gardens. Sometimes I'm so lonely that the marble statues seem to move in the corner of my eye, but as soon as I look, they freeze back into stone.

The cat the Marquis gave me has run away. Even she found it too lonely in this haunted castle.

Everyone leaves me behind.

For three months, I haven't had any appetite. The Marquis didn't take me as his wife, but as his prisoner.

I am no longer allowed to leave the grounds, Rousel says. On his master's orders. It's too dangerous for me to be out alone.

They all act as if they care about my safety. In truth, they're just afraid I might run away and never return.

I'm a pretty piece in the Marquis' collection, slowly gathering dust and losing significance.

I am nothing.
I am nobody.
I am alone.

THIRTY-TWO

Charlotte and I have made peace. Our arguments always go the same way. We yell at each other, we don't speak for a while, until one of us shows up at the other's door and apologizes with a silent hug.

This time, my sister took the first step, even though I can't blame her for being upset. If my life were at stake, it would be hard for me to remain composed as well.

It's almost ironic that the Marquis has provided me with my own parlor, while there's no one left who could visit me except Charlotte.

Mother still doesn't leave the house, my friends haven't been in touch since I got married, out of fear of the Marquis, and I ignore Gabriel's calls to spare him from a terrible fate.

After my husband warned me not to get close to another man ever again (even platonically), I don't dare to speak to my childhood friend anymore.

"Where is your hot husband off to?" Charlotte sips her tea and burns the tip of her tongue. "Ouch!"

"That's what you get for asking silly questions."

"I don't know what you're talking about," she replies with an innocent face.

"I've told you ten times already that he's traveling. Don't you think if we had been in touch, I would have told you?"

"Ah, touchy subject, I see. Do you miss him?"

I look out the window at the horses in the paddock. Ombre is grazing contentedly. How I wish I could trade places with him.

"I miss human contact. I miss the feeling of having a family."

"And they say money makes you happy." Charlotte sets her cup down. "I understand you, Louise. Really. All jokes aside - I always assumed that the Marquis would take you with him on his travels. I couldn't have imagined in my wildest dreams that he would just leave you to die from boredom and not even allow you to leave the grounds. Is that even legal?"

I chuckle. "The newspaper said he was attending a horse race with the Prime Minister last week. I think he holds all the cards if I were to take him to court."

"You're right," she says, chewing on her thumbnail. "But you can't live locked up in this castle for the rest of your life, while your husband's only paying you a formal visit every six months."

"You can't even call it a visit. We eat silently next to each other, and he checks the stock market on his phone."

"I had so much hope," she sighs. "Somehow, I believed that your story would turn out well."

"This is real life. Villains don't become heroes like in fairy tales," I reply.

She shakes her head. "I could swear, the way he looked at you at the wedding, up there at the altar, that there was something more. He always has such an incredibly cold gaze, but when you walked towards him... he looked different. Like a real human being."

I don't want to hear this. I don't want to hope that the Marquis could develop feelings for me. It's enough that I dream at night of being touched by him.

"He's playing with me."

"How so?"

To distract my trembling hands, I put more sugar into my tea.

"He kissed me."

"He did what?!"

"And right after, he left. That was over three months ago. He kissed me and then ghosted me. I think he regrets it."

Charlotte runs her hands through her hair in excitement. "Oh my God. That changes everything. He's into you! I knew it."

I would love to jump up and cover her mouth, like we used to do as kids when one of us got on the other's nerves.

"It didn't mean anything. I think he was just carried away because he felt sorry for me. We had just been talking about how I gave up my dream of competitive riding, and somehow it just happened."

"How does he kiss?"

"Charlotte..."

"Don't keep me in suspense like this."

"Okay. He kisses okay."

Like a thousand dreams I didn't know lived in my heart. Like lips that touch not just the skin, but the depths of the soul. Like sweet promises in which I lose myself forever and thirst that can only be quenched by his breath.

If I could, I would repeat the kiss immediately. The Marquis revealed so much to me without words. That he wants to dominate and possess me, that he wants to teach me how to love and reveal a world to me that would forever remain hidden from me without him.

But I can't enjoy the memory of his kiss. The realization that he doesn't feel the same weighs too heavily on me, because if he had enjoyed our touch, he wouldn't be on the run now. He can't look me in the eyes because he's ashamed of himself.

"For someone who kisses just okay, you're blushing quite a lot. I'm so proud of myself, my gut feeling didn't deceive me. I'm telling you, he has a huge dick, a million percent."

I bite my tongue in shock. "Charlotte!" A door slams shut. We both startle.

"What was that?" I jump up and quickly walk in the direction of the sound. I can't find anything unusual. There's no one here. The suspicion in my chest remains as I return to Charlotte.

"I think someone was eavesdropping on us."

"Nonsense. Who?"

"I don't know." Or - I don't want to know, because there is a person in this house whom I fear more than the Marquis, a person who hates me and is working with all their might to get rid of me. She has blonde hair and is the definition of beauty. I stand no chance against her.

THIRTY-THREE

Spring is creeping in quietly. The birds start singing earlier in the morning. Cool silk sheets cling to my naked skin.

I sigh contentedly. Only in sleep do I find peace. In my dreams, the Marquis touches me in every possible way.

Something vibrates. Half asleep, I sit up. The bright light of my phone screen burns into my eyes, still accustomed to the darkness of early morning.

The caller doesn't give up. I reach for the phone that the Marquis gave me. Only he has my number…

"Hello?" I answer with a rough voice.

"Hello Louise, how are you?"

Hearing him speak after so long gets under my skin. It's one thing to remember a person. You can summon words and interactions, but the face blurs over time and memories gradually feel like elusive ghosts. But a smell or the sound of a voice brings back everything you thought you had forgotten.

"You're not dead yet?" I ask outright. "By now, I expected to inherit a fortune and go down in history as the youngest widow in France."

"Believe me, there are many who lost their husbands earlier."

"Did they poison him?"

"You'll have to come up with your own ideas if

you want to get rid of me. Use that creative little brain of yours. But please, no poison. That would be too mundane, and I would take it as an insult."

He always manages to disarm me. Every. Damn. Time.

"Why are you calling?"

"No specific reason. I just wanted to hear how you're doing. What you've been up to."

"And why exactly should it matter to you?"

He remains silent for a second too long.

"You are my wife."

"On paper."

"I promised to take care of you."

"To kiss me, leave me standing, and fly to another continent is an interesting way of taking care of someone."

"I have obligations. You know that."

"I don't believe a word you say. You left because you lost control and regret our kiss. Just admit it."

"Do *you* regret it?" His question catches me off guard. I have to swallow hard.

I could lie, or… "No. I don't regret it," my heart decides and speaks for me.

"Why not?"

I realize that I shouldn't trust him, that the price of my honest words will be high. The Marquis is a deadly weapon. Not because he's influential and ruthless, but because he makes you forget how destructive his touch can be.

He is the dagger I plunge into my own heart

without him even having to lift a finger.

He plays on the fact that he looks good, that his lips bring ruin but taste like dreams from which you wake too soon and desperately try to return.

"Your kiss betrayed you. That's why I don't regret it."

"Explain that to me."

"Why should I?"

"I'm bored, and you're lonely. Neither of us has anything better to do right now."

Sleep is out of the question. Defeated, I sit up in my bed and switch on the lamp on my nightstand.

"You act as if I don't matter to you. As if I were a burden that my father has punished you with and that you're tired of carrying. But that's not true. I've seen through you. Your lips gave it away. Your kiss was too hungry to have been just a game."

He laughs. "You amuse me, Louise. Truly. You have a talent for stringing words together and make them sound believable. But unfortunately, I must disappoint you. The reason I kissed you had nothing to do with hidden affection."

Instinctively, I cross my arms over my chest while balancing the phone on my naked, trembling knees.

"I kissed you to shut you up. I rarely encounter people like you. Most of the people I deal with know their limits. They know when it's better to keep quiet. Coming from a respected family, I assumed you had been taught manners. But when you're upset, you talk and talk and talk without stopping, and this lack of control goes against everything I stand for."

My stomach tightens. "In short, I'm a pain in the ass."

"That's what you said."

We both fall silent. I still haven't understood why he wants to talk to me.

Is he lonely?

Does he worry about me?

Does he want to torment me?

"The kiss meant nothing. You should forget it. In the future, I will find better ways to silence you."

"Or, you listen to my opinions and realize that even little foolish girls occasionally have something meaningful to say."

Silence.

"Any news about Charlotte? Has anyone else come to mind who she could marry? Someone influential enough to protect her from Gino?"

The Marquis could be hiding in any hidden corner of the world at this moment. Maybe he will never come back. My stomach rebels against the feeling that I depend on his help.

"You know, Louise, I like you. Even though you drive me crazy sometimes. You fight for what's important to you, and I appreciate that. But I've realized a few things during my trip."

I swallow. I know I'm not prepared for what's coming next.

"I have given you too much importance. Our wedding should have been a formality, a signature, a promise fulfilled. Instead, I made your problems mine and tried to carry some of your burdens for you. That was a mistake."

"You did what? Giving me importance? Locking me up in a castle, disappearing for months, and sleeping with another woman... that's what you call giving importance?"

"Jealous, little one?" His voice is sweet as honey and poisonous as the bite of a deadly viper.

"Oh sure. I've always wanted to lose my heart to a cold businessman who'd sell me into human trafficking without batting an eye. Because that's exactly what you do, don't you? You make people your pawns, figures on a chessboard designed to let you win every time. You don't care about anyone. Not even yourself. You only love your wealth and the feeling of being destructive. But in the end, that will be your downfall, and you'll feel alone, terribly alone."

His silence could mean anything. It drives me crazy that it's always impossible to know where I stand with him.

"You're strong", he finally says.

"I know."

"But not strong enough to stay away from me."

My tongue sticks dry to my teeth. My heart races faster than the Marquis's most expensive horses.

"I've changed my mind, little one. I'm going to leave you to your fate. It was fun playing with your hope, and who knows, in another life, I might have even saved your sister. But I don't feel like it anymore. I'm bored. I want to find out what your tears taste like when your little heart breaks forever. I want to look into your eyes when you lose your sister for good."

And he hangs up.

THIRTY-FOUR

I am many things. I am a naive girl who dreams of big things, of angels protecting me in my sleep and princes rescuing me from abandoned castles.

I am a prisoner slowly being forgotten by the world outside.

I am a virgin whose only kiss was a lie.

But one thing I am not. A coward.

The Marquis will choke on his arrogance. He will freeze in his cold lonely bed when Madison finally realizes she loves a monster. He will forget my name and forget that I was ever part of his life.

I trusted him. Because he was the only person I could transform into a hero in my imagination, even though everything spoke against him saving my family.

His shoulders seemed strong and his straight posture determined enough to let me get lost in the illusion that he would fight for the woman he promised to protect.

I shouldn't be angry with him. I should only hate myself for letting myself be so quickly blinded by his golden smile, by his breathtaking beauty.

It was all my mistake.

But Charlotte's life won't save itself, especially if I continue to wait for a miracle to happen. If I don't take matters into my own hands to free us from the disastrous situation Albert has put us in, then no one will.

We are alone, but therein lies our strength. We don't have to consider anyone else. My fighting spirit is awakened – and my thirst for revenge.

Perhaps it's time for traditions to be forgotten and the powerful men of our world to become mere memories with no voice. Maybe it's time for us to start speaking.

With confident movements, I pack my clothes into the suitcase that I brought with me when I moved in. The Marquis has bought me so many dresses during these past months I lived with him that I can't possibly take my entire wardrobe, so I pack what is practical, comfortable, and inconspicuous.

A shadow moves in the corner of my eye. I startle.

Madison leans in the doorway, grinning at me. "I didn't think I'd get rid of you so early, and above all, I was convinced it would require much more effort on my part. But it looks like you're smarter than I assumed and are clearing the field on your own."

Her arrogance makes me sick. "Yes, Madison, we've all got it. You're the untouchable queen, the one who's in charge here. Swallow it and just be happy that you've won."

A furrow appears between her eyebrows, but the rest of her face doesn't betray her true feelings as she speaks calmly.

"You don't really think the Marquis will just let you go, do you?"

I would love to cover my ears, but both my hands are busy squeezing my favorite books into the already full suitcase. I don't want to leave anything behind that's important to me, not a single part of myself. The Marquis and his gloomy castle should forget me forever. As if I had never existed. A shadow in magnificent corridors. A quiet sob breaking through the night.

"I don't care about the Marquis. You can have him."

She laughs. Her laughter is more unsettling than her anger. It's more unpredictable and insidious. It doesn't reveal what comes next.

"But that's not how it works. Even though I'm glad you realize how dispensable you are in this house, it almost gives me even more pleasure to watch you walk into your own downfall. What do you think the Marquis will do when he finds out that you're not following his orders, that you're leaving the estate against his will and trying to escape?"

"I don't matter to him."

"That's not important. You belong to him. He never gives back what was given to him. Or sold."

I angrily let go of my suitcase, its zipper on the verge of bursting, plant my hands on my hips, and raise my voice. "Do you even listen to yourself? I'm not some soulless object to be passed from one owner to another and left behind in dusty rooms. I am a human being. With feelings - and free will. If I want to leave, I will leave. If I want a divorce, then I will get one. Ten Marquises can't stop me."

It unsettles me that she remains calm and continues to smile, but I have no time to waste. I need to get out of here. I have no idea when my husband will return. It could be in a year or in two minutes. One thing is certain - I need to disappear from here before he shows up and cuts off my escape forever.

"A marriage contract is a purchase agreement. You can try to convince yourself otherwise, but that doesn't change the facts. The Marquis will unfortunately bring you back. I hope he does it with anger. I hope he hurts you."

I must not let her provoke me. She wants to torment me. Knowing that any angry reaction from me will only encourage her to continue shooting her poisoned arrows in my direction, I remain silent and throw my full body weight onto the suitcase. Finally, the zipper gives way and I am ready to leave.

Madison stands in the doorway.

"Let me pass."

"Don't you want to say goodbye to me? The next time I see you, you could be dead."

"Let's hope so," I hiss and push past her. She is less strong than she looks.

Love doesn't conquer fear. Hope doesn't conquer fear. Action does.

I can't go to my old home. It's the first place the Marquis will look for me. There's only one place where he won't be able to find me.

"Louise?" Gabriel's eyes light up with surprise as he sees me.

A flash of lightning illuminates the sky above us. I'm drenched from having to walk, the rain whipping against my face.

"Come in quickly, or you'll catch a cold." His embrace is the comfort that the world has denied me for months. An apology that I now realize I deserve.

The guesthouse smells of freshly baked apple pie. Gabriel has a passion for pastries. Although he still lives on his parents' estate, after turning eighteen he moved to the family's somewhat secluded guesthouse. A golf course and a private park separate him from his sisters' prying eyes and his mother's judging gaze.

I didn't announce my arrival because I was afraid he might deny me entry and not take me in. The Marquis made it clear what he thought of our friendship during their last encounter.

But Gabriel is reliable, a loyal companion who would never abandon his friends for anything in the world.

As I step into his living room, I struggle to hold back the tears that cloud my vision. Everything is so familiar, so warm, that my chest tightens.

Gabriel is still living the life that I have lost forever.

"What happened?" he asks, concerned, taking my luggage. "Sit down. Shall I make you some tea?"

"No, thank you."

"But at least a glass of water. You look horrible. Did you walk all the way here?"

I nod, my teeth chattering.

"Did the Marquis run out of money for gas? I knew the fuel prices were high, but I didn't realize the situation was that serious…"

His attempt at a joke makes me smile. Gabriel is the only person who will still make me laugh on my deathbed. Everything about him is caring and understanding.

"I've missed you so much."

"I've missed you too."

"And I'm sorry I neglected you. He didn't allow me to reach out to you."

"It's okay. It doesn't matter. I know how the game works. The Marquis's wife shouldn't have male friends, it's not proper."

We both roll our eyes. We both despise the outdated rules of this world.

"I don't want you to think I'm only coming to you because I have no other place to hide. I'm here because you're the only person I trust. Besides Charlotte, of course."

"Hide?"

Damn it. I bite my tongue until it bleeds. Why can't I think before speaking and choose my words more wisely?

"Don't tell me you're hiding from him. You know I can't protect you here."

Fear flickers in his caramel-brown eyes. He would

never abandon me, but he's also just a human, and nobody wants to be an enemy of the Marquis.

"Has he…" - his voice trembles - "has he hurt you?"

"Yes, but…" His hands clench into fists. "Not like you think. Just with words. He doesn't hit women."

At least not unless they ask for it. I quickly push away the memory of what I heard from his bedroom when Madison spent the night with him.

"What did he do then? Why are you here?"

"It's so stupid." I stare at my hands.

"None of your feelings are stupid. Especially not when he has hurt you, Louise."

He's right.

I take a deep breath. "He kissed me, only to tell me afterwards that it meant nothing, that it was a mistake. But that's not why I fled."

A rumble of thunder interrupts me. Three breaths. Blood rushing in my ears. Gabriel's concerned look, comforting me.

"He had promised me to find a man for Charlotte who would protect her life from Gino. You know, he wants to take revenge on us."

Gabriel just nods with his mouth open. The weight of my words is clearly visible on him.

"He assured me that he would find a solution. But instead, he called me this morning to tell me that he's leaving me to my fate and… and… will watch as my heart breaks." A sob escapes me. All the pain, all the many little stabs that I have suppressed, they overwhelm me. My dreams are forever carried away by a wave of despair.

Gabriel moves closer and puts an arm around my shoulder.

"I'm so ashamed."

He kisses my temple in a brotherly way. "Don't you dare make yourself small just because that jerk feels intimidated by your greatness. You've done nothing wrong."

"But I… I like him."

Now it's out. The stupid, stupid words that I've hoped would suffocate me in my sleep. The dreams that keep me awake night after night. The memory of his gentle touch, when for a moment he convinced me that he meant it. When his eyes looked like they could only tell the truth.

"That's not your fault either. Have you seen the guy? He looks dangerously good. Believe me, if I could, I'd take him from behind for nights on end."

"Gabriel!"

"It's just the truth. What I'm trying to say is, of course, you're attracted to him. It would be strange if you weren't. He dresses well, he looks incredibly good, he's powerful, strong, confident… Men like him should be kept captive in books. It shouldn't even be possible for them to really exist. Doesn't that contradict some physical law of nature?"

I tiredly rest my head on his shoulder. He strokes my hair. "You're staying here with me now. For as long as you want. No one can find you here. Gino doesn't know me. I'm too small and insignificant for the Marquis to even consider showing up here. My home is now your hideout. And as for your feelings, they will pass. Trust me, you just need to give your heart time. Your true love is still out there waiting for you."

"Promise?"

"I swear."

In Gabriel's guest room, I finally find true peace for the first time in weeks. The fatigue leaves my bones.

In the morning, I open my eyes feeling refreshed. After a long shower, I'm reborn.

Gabriel makes us breakfast. I chew on the strawberry roll, which tastes of hope, and stir sugar into my coffee.

Gabriel is in the middle of telling me the latest gossip from my former group of friends when we are interrupted by a buzzing sound coming from my room.

"Oh no, no no no no - it's my phone!"

This can't be happening. I left it on the bed before grabbing my suitcase and leaving my chambers. The Marquis himself told me that he can track me at any time through the GPS. That's why it was so important not to take it with me.

Anxiously, I walk towards the buzzing sound. There's a light flashing in the outer pocket of my backpack. With trembling fingers, I open the bag and pull out the cursed device. His name is displayed on the screen. He knows that I've fled.

"Is everything okay?" Gabriel asks.

"No, not at all. I have no idea how…" But I do. There is an explanation. "Madison must have quickly slipped it into my bag as I passed by her. She knew the Marquis would be able to find me that way."

"But what does she gain from this? Shouldn't she be glad to be rid of you?"

"She knows he'll be furious. I think she enjoys watching him punish me. She wants to see him hate me."

I have to swallow hard. Breakfast is out of the question now.

"Gabriel, I'm so grateful that you let me sleep here, but I have to leave. It's only a matter of time before he shows up at the door."

"But where will you go?"

"I will get a hotel room, book a flight, and hide somewhere he can't find me."

"Do you need cash?" Gabriel is one step ahead of me. Of course, the Marquis has likely already blocked my cards.

But before I can answer, there's a knock on the door. Once, then again and again, determined and angry.

"Damn it."

THIRTY-FIVE

"Get out through the kitchen window. I'll distract him."

"Okay." I hug Gabriel tightly. "Thank you for everything."

Another knock. The intervals are getting shorter. Just a few more breaths and he will break down the door.

BANG BANG BANG.

"Go!" Gabriel releases me and pushes me towards the kitchen. I throw my backpack over my shoulder and run. The suitcase has to stay behind, even though it will betray me. If the Marquis sees my things, he will know I was here, but I can't think about that now. I can't afford to lose time. Maybe I'm being silly. Who knows if he's even angry? Maybe I don't matter to him and am overestimating my importance. Maybe it doesn't matter if I'm gone.

BANG BANG BANG.

The blows against the front door tell a different story. *If* it's even him standing there. Perhaps it's just Gabriel's father, who has something important to tell him?

"Where is my wife?" No. Clearly, it's his voice.

"Calm down, she's not here," I hear Gabriel speaking from a distance. You can tell he's lying. I know the Marquis sees through him. I try to open the window. It's stuck. Oh my God.

"You have three seconds to get out of my way. Otherwise, I can't guarantee anything."

"She's not here!"

"Two seconds and I'll put a fucking bullet between your eyes."

Gabriel doesn't give in. I hear a thud and my friend's startled cry. I can't leave him behind. Not like this. I take a deep breath, summoning all the courage that remains.

The Marquis is still standing in the doorway, but Gabriel is on the ground. A gash on his head glows red. His eyelids flutter.

"What have you done?!" I scream.

The Marquis just looks at me silently. His face is expressionless, almost bored.

"Who the hell do you think you are?" he growls calmly.

I want to answer, but I can't. My mouth is dry as dust.

"ANSWER ME."

"I have nothing more to say to you. I don't know what you want to hear from me."

"Better come up with something quickly."

"You left me behind. You were just gone. I felt so alone. I... I couldn't. I went to find Gabriel because..."

"Because?" he urges, his nostrils flaring.

"Because I was damn lonely," I scream in his beautiful face. "I'm not a painting that you hang on the wall in one of your precious rooms and occasionally look at. I am a human being! Not a fucking pet!"

"You're right. Because a pet would have more loyalty than you, fucking whore," he spits.

I take in a sharp breath of the cold spring air through my teeth.

"This marriage is over. I will leave you."

"Oh no," his jaw twitches. "This marriage has only just begun."

His dark silhouette is so tall that he has to duck as he steps through the doorway and slowly approaches me. "You made a mistake, Louise, a reckless mistake. So far, I've held back for the sake of your youth. But it seems you're not the innocent girl you pretended to be. Now you will truly get to know me."

His hand moves too quickly to my face. He presses a piece of wet cloth against my mouth.

Everything goes black. My heart, my soul, his smile as he catches me and I fall, fall, fall.

THIRTY-SIX

The clock is ticking too loudly. I try to open my mouth, try to speak and order someone to remove it from the room. But my lips are so dry, my throat so rough, that I can't make a sound. Water. I need water.

THIRTY-SEVEN

His steps are circling me. His gaze burns into my skin. I can feel him standing in front of my bed, even though it's too dark to really see anything and my eyelids flutter.

"Where am I?"

"In safety."

Liar.

Traitor.

Marquis.

THIRTY-EIGHT

It could have been hours or days when I open my eyes. My head is too heavy for my neck. I stay lying down. Everything is spinning.

Painted naked angels smile down at me from the ornate ceiling. I don't know if they want to show compassion or mock me, but they betray where I am. In the Marquis' bedroom.

I've only been there once, when I was spying, and I never dared to go near his rooms again.

"Are you thirsty?"

I startle. With all the strength left in me, I lift my head. He sits at the foot of the bed on a baroque chair, watching me.

"What have you done?"

"Brought you home. Where you belong."

"Yes."

"Pardon?"

"Yes, I am thirsty."

Without hesitation, he rises and strides towards me. Because I'm too weak to hold the crystal glass myself, he brings it to my lips and supports my head as I drink greedily.

He has to refill it twice before my thirst is finally quenched.

I'm feeling better already. Suspiciously, I sit up and lean against the headboard. The Marquis sits down next to me on the mattress and looks at me.

"Did you drug me?" Why else would I not remember anything? I can't recall a single memory of how I got back to the castle.

"Yes. You were too rebellious, Louise. I didn't want to hurt you, and I knew you would resist physically."

"You're sick."

"Tell me something I don't know."

I want to wipe the smirk off his face. Never before have I hated a person as much as I do in this moment.

"What about Gabriel? Is he okay?"

"Don't worry. I had my doctor come before I left with you. Only when it was certain that your... friend was in stable condition did I leave him. Even though, for what he did, he deserved to die, right?"

I gasp. "If you harm him in any way, I will kill you."

His smirk widens. His hand touches my forehead and runs through my hair, as gently as a butterfly's wing.

Angry, I hit his arm. "Gabriel helped me."

"Wrong. He encouraged you to make a mistake. He tried to keep you away from your husband."

"He took me in when I had nowhere else to go."

"You can always come to me. You will always have a safe place by my side."

"You are dangerous."

"I'll never be a danger to you. Only to your heart."

I bite my lower lip until my mouth tastes of iron. "You just disappeared. Without a word. I had almost forgotten what you looked like. I couldn't remember the sound of your voice - and when you finally felt it necessary to contact me, all you had to say was pure pain."

Something flickers in the green of his eyes. A shadow that I can't grasp and that dissipates too quickly. I want to call it back, but I don't know how.

"I feel nothing for you, Louise. You have to accept that."

Why does he constantly portray me as a lovesick girl who has lost her head for him, when the truth couldn't be further from it? He is the embodiment of arrogance. My fingernails dig into the silk of the bed sheets.

"But that doesn't mean I can disregard the rules. These rules state that I have rightfully taken you as my wife. What do you think it will look like if you run away?"

"People will say that you're weak and have no control over me."

"Exactly."

"What's so bad about the truth?"

His nostrils flare.

"It's true. You *are* weak. But not because I resist you, but because you deny your true feelings."

"Mind your tongue."

"I felt it. I understood what you were trying to tell me when your lips pressed so hungrily against mine."

I free myself from the bedcovers. With each word I speak, I lean closer to him. "You wonder how the other parts of my body taste, the hidden ones. You imagine how my voice sounds when I sigh your name. You become hard when you watch me walking in front of you. Admit it, all-powerful Marquis - the real reason you brought me back is because you can't stop dreaming of fucking me."

His face remains cold and noble, but the air around us changes its shape. It thickens. It becomes harder to breathe, and my chest rises and falls faster.

He doesn't move. He lurks. "Is this what you're after, little one? Is that why you ran away? So I would bring you back and make you come?"

I hit a sore spot.

"Were you really willing to leave this life behind?" His large hand gestures in a circle, encompassing the opulent room. "Horses and limousines and every desire fulfilled with a snap of the fingers? All the beautiful things I've given you? What would you have traded them for, Louise?"

He really thinks he has figured me out.

"My heart doesn't cling to material things."

"Oh no, Louise, it doesn't. But it clings to me."

My breath catches. His index finger touches my mouth. Slowly, he begins to trace the contour of my lips. "You can't stop thinking about our kiss. Because you've never had a strong man in your life. You always had to be strong for everyone. For your mother, to whom you were never perfect enough. For your sister, whose life you try to save. For your father, who only played the role of the head of the family but was never brave enough to actually stand up for you. You long to be protected. You yearn for me to kiss away the melancholy that has accompanied you all your life."

His eyes darken like the night. I've never noticed how long his dark eyelashes really are.

"Deep down inside, you know that we would be perfect for each other. Your hopeful nature and my strong back. You would help me rediscover faith in the world, true joy in life, and I would protect you from all the dangers out there. That's what you want. Admit it, Louise."

His words have sucked the breath from my lungs. My stomach shrinks. The boundaries of my body dissolve.

"No. I don't want you."

"You need to learn to lie better, my dear."

In a desperate attempt to regain control, I bring my face even closer to his. "You want me so much that it drives you crazy."

"If that were true," he growls, "I would have taken you already."

He lunges forward, I lose my balance and fall backward onto the mattress. His warm, hard body hovers closely over me, he supports himself with both arms next to my head.

His breath smells sweet, of fulfilled desires and fire and predestined love.

"Be careful, Louise. You think you want me. But you don't know what it would really mean to love someone like me. Don't do this to yourself."

"Just one night," I say and grab his shoulders so he can't escape, although it's a ridiculous attempt given his strong muscles that could easily crush me.

"I want to know what it feels like to be touched. Truly touched."

His mouth hardens.

"Show me how it feels. Just once. I don't want to live and die as a virgin."

He didn't expect that - and although his face remains impassive, and I can't see the slightest hint of nervousness in him, even though he remains the cold, perfect statue he always is, his body betrays him. A part of him gives him away. His hard erection presses into my stomach.

He's big. Too big.

Wordless seconds pass. Centuries pass us by. Nothing matters except the two square meters my life has shrunk to as the man I once feared lies on top of me, the man my body now craves.

When he pulls away from me, it feels like he's taking a part of me with him. He straightens his jacket. In control as always. Unreachable as ever.

"I will think about it. Until then, show me what a good girl you can be. I have a weakness for good girls."

The door slams shut behind him. A common thread runs through all our encounters - he leaves me unsatisfied and hungry for more every time.

A NOBLE CONTRACT

THIRTY-NINE

After we touched each other like lovers for the second time, the Marquis is more distant than ever.

I know how to keep myself occupied. Although he disapproves of me working in the stables, I love the smell of straw and the snorting of the horses too much to let him stop me. My riding boots are caked with mud. I stomp a few times to shake off the worst before entering the entrance hall of the castle.

Charlotte is probably waiting for me already. She promised to be here this afternoon to take a walk with me in the gardens and tell me what Mother does behind closed doors all day.

I hurry up the wide, curving marble staircase towards my chambers. From a distance, I can already hear agitated voices. *One* agitated voice. The second sounds calm and composed. A man and a woman.

For a moment, I want to believe that it's Madison and the Marquis having one of their constant arguments as of late. But the voices are coming from my chambers, and that doesn't make sense. Why would they settle for my rooms when they have an entire suite to themselves?

The staff never argue. The Marquis's servants are masters at making themselves invisible.

As I'm almost at the door leading to my rooms, I freeze. The female voice says my name.

"If Louise finds out...".

"She won't, I'll make sure of it."

Charlotte. It's Charlotte speaking and... the Marquis.

Curiosity burns in my heart, but I shouldn't eavesdrop on my own sister. It feels wrong to hold my breath so she doesn't hear that I'm nearby.

Determined, I push the door open. What I see shocks me deeply. The Marquis has grabbed Charlotte's arm and is pressing her with his full body weight against a bookshelf, which is already dangerously swaying.

Her determined almond-shaped eyes, so similar to mine, glare at him. Before either of them can say another word, I step in.

"Let her go immediately! Or I'll call the police."

The Marquis freezes. Slowly, he turns his head and looks at me, but he remains in his tense position and doesn't release Charlotte.

"What is going on here?" I ask with a trembling voice, and as he notices my eyes beginning to fill with tears, he releases his grip. Angrily, Charlotte shakes her arm as if trying to get the blood flowing again and adjusts her blouse.

"You uncouth bastard. A man of class, you say? I'm ashamed of you." My sister's words bounce off the Marquis, just as it seems mine never have an effect on him.

My protective instinct is awakened. Concerned, I approach my sister and embrace her. She returns my hug, and I'm on the verge of spitting in the Marquis's face, but I won't give him the satisfaction of losing control.

"How dare you touch her like this? Has the devil possessed you?" I ask angrily.

"He *is* the devil," Charlotte hisses.

He clears his throat. "Louise, I need to talk to you. Alone."

"Why? To feed her lies? To manipulate her?"

Charlotte looks at me with flushed cheeks. "He wants to drive a wedge between us. He wants to distance you from anyone who matters to you and who could open your eyes when he mistreats you."

The Marquis exhales loudly and runs his hand along his face. He has negotiated with the toughest, most powerful men in the world, but two young women in their early twenties are testing his patience.

"He tried to force me to promise not to visit you anymore," Charlotte blurts out.

"That's not true," he says calmly. Too calmly. It scares me. Only a psychopath could remain so unaffected in such an emotionally charged situation.

"Oh yes, it *is* true," she says, raising a threatening finger. I've never seen her so upset. He must have really hit a nerve with her. "He said that I was a bad influence on you, that I would put foolish ideas in your head, and that you could never get used to a life with him if I kept interfering."

He grins, but it's not an amused grin, it's a deadly one. His lips move in a way that makes me fear he could snap my sister's neck and let her bleed out on one of his expensive carpets at any moment.

"You have quite the imagination. I'll give you that," his voice suddenly sounds foreign to me. When he seeks my gaze, I instinctively look away.

"You have to believe me, Louise, that's not what happened. It's more serious than you can imagine. I need to talk to you."

My eyes strain as they shift from one to the other, from my sister's trembling chin to the tense shoulders of my husband, who is a stranger to me... and always will be.

I can't see behind his mask, but I know who my sister is and that she would never lie to me, no matter what happens.

"Out," I say softly but firmly. "Disappear immidiately and do not return to my chambers ever again."

"Louise," he takes a helpless step towards me. I have actually managed to unsettle him, but my victory doesn't feel like a victory.

"I take it all back. Every word, every plea. None of it matters anymore. From now on, we only speak when absolutely necessary. No one hurts my sister. Do you understand?"

He takes a deep breath. "You will regret this," he says and turns away from me, heading towards the door. He pauses briefly as if he wants to say something else, but then changes his mind and disappears.

You will regret this. My gut feeling remains silent as I wonder whether it was a threat or an prediction of the future.

FORTY

The Marquis hosts three balls a year. Those who receive an invitation live a carefree life. Those, like me, who are forced to attend can resist as much as they want, but they cannot escape the one overshadowing truth: the Marquis dictates the course of events.

His noose tightened around my neck the day my father accepted his offer, and I was too blind to realize how it slowly constricted.

As I lean on the railing of the golden balcony overlooking the ballroom, I can't take my eyes off him. The Marquis is dancing with Madison. He leads her, just as he led me when we danced together months ago.

She looks up at him, as I looked up at him when I believed that his word meant something.

He has forbidden Charlotte from accompanying me. She is not allowed to set foot on his property, and knowing her, her proud spirit and stubborn soul, she wouldn't do it even if he allowed her to.

The Colbert family has been hosting the most opulent parties in the country for centuries, ones that would make the Sun King pale in comparison, with decadent mountains of delicacies, cascades of flowing champagne, and women so beautiful they freeze the breath in my lungs.

The Marquis has given me another useless dress that will gather dust in my closet.

He didn't listen to me when I screamed after him that I wouldn't dream of showing up by his side tonight. He escorted me out of my room, grabbed my hand, and wrapped himself around me like a dark shadow, directing me up the red-carpeted stairs and placing me in the royal box.

After he disappeared without a word, my first impuls was to flee. But he is clever. He knows me by now. He locked the door, and now I stand alone in a box, looking down on the dancing crowd.

My heart constricts as he brushes a strand of hair from Madison's face. If only he weren't so beautiful. If only everything didn't push me in his direction, all the invisible forces and hands of hell that render me powerless and whisper to me to seek his closeness.

A man catches my gaze. He appears at the edge of the dance floor, dressed in dark, expensive but noticeably simple fabrics. It's clear that he didn't choose his suit for this event; rather, he seems lost and searching. He reminds me of a younger version of the Marquis, but more restless. His blonde hair is perfectly styled, and he's tall.

He circles the dancers, lurking. He moves in my direction, but he can't see me since I'm outside his field of vision, high up in the air. It's as if an invisible web, woven from the tears of ancient myths, surrounds him, separating him from ordinary mortals.

He doesn't notice anyone. His gaze is fixed on one person: my husband. The Marquis has come to a stop beneath my box. If I listen closely, I can hear his voice.

The stranger pushes past well-dressed guests, men who seem to recognize him. He ignores them all and approaches the Marquis. The Marquis feels his gaze. He looks up at him. His body freezes. Only his lips move as he says, "Roman."

And then he embraces him in a way I've never seen him touch anyone before, so honest and warm that it makes me sick because I want to be the one who brings a smile to his stony face.

The rest of their brief conversation blurs with the murmur of the crowd, with laughter and classical music. The Marquis places his hand on his friend's upper arm. They disappear behind a door. Curiosity overwhelms me from behind.

I'm not proud of my work as the historical door lock breaks. It hurts me in my heart to destroy such an old door, but I need to get out of this lodge.

As I gather the red stiff silk of my gown and hurry down a flight of stairs, I try to convince myself that I'm spying on him out of boredom, that he's the only pastime offered to me in this dreary cage of gold.

It's a lie.

I've had enough of the Marquis leading a secret life behind my back. His secrets are eating me up.

He fascinates me. I want to know what he discusses behind closed doors. I want to understand him.

An elegant hand closes a door. I would recognize these fingers anywhere; the feeling of their touch is seared into my memory.

My original plan was to follow the two men into their hiding room, but now I realize how naive of a thought that is, as they would immediately discover me and interrupt their conversation. So I have no choice but to press my ear against the door and hope that nobody discovers me.

"If he sees you, it's over for you. Don't you understand that?"

"I had to let you know that I'm alive. He's always one step ahead of me. I had no way to call you or write to you without him being able to track me."

"And you think it's smart to show up here, to walk right into the hornet's nest and appear where he is?"

"The only place he doesn't expect me is right behind him. You know him. You know how he is. He's so trapped in his delusions of grandeur that he believes I'm afraid of him and hiding. He would never think that I'm in the same room as him."

"You've lost your mind, Roman."

"I was born without a mind. That's what connects us."

"Wrong. Many things connect us, but I would never recklessly put my life on the line as you do."

"It's not just about me anymore."

"Don't say it."

"I've fallen in love - and I have to protect her from

him."

With bated breath, I open the slightly ajar door. The Marquis and his friend stand facing each other closely. They are almost the same height, the Marquis towering over him by only a few millimeters.

"Will you introduce me to the lady sometime? I would like to express my condolences to her."

"What about you, Jerome?" the stranger grins. His eyes betray that he fears no one.

"How's life as a married man? I regret not having been able to attend your wedding."

"That's what it's like when you're on the run."

As I feel that I've been holding my breath for too long, that I'm starting to feel nauseous, I attempt to breathe in quietly, but my instincts have a way of their own and a loud noise escapes my throat.

Faster than fear, the Marquis turns around. He immediately spots me, as if an invisible thread connects us. His look becomes angrier, but for a moment I think I see a hint of relief in it.

"What the hell are *you* doing here?"

"I was curious," I try with the truth. He grabs my wrist, pulls me into the room and leans his back against the door so that no one can surprise us.

His hand grabs my chin. He tilts my head, forcing me to look at him.

"What did I tell you about spying?" He seems not to notice how he's running his tongue over his lips - and that it drives me crazy.

The stranger laughs behind us. "Nice to see that

you haven't changed."

The Marquis lets go of my chin. I rub my aching jaw.

"Has she not yet succeeded in melting your heart of ice?" The stranger seems to revel in making things awkward.

The Marquis closes his eyes for a moment, as if he needs to gather himself internally to avoid committing murder. When he opens them again, he seems transformed. He speaks in a calmer voice, and once again I wonder how many different versions of himself he carries within.

"Roman, this is Louise. My wife."

Roman makes a mocking gesture and a cruel smile flits over his beautiful lips. "Pleased to meet you."

"Save your breath," the Marquis interrupts him. "Louise, this is Roman van den Berg. My brother."

"Half-brother," Roman grins, and the resemblance leaves me speechless.

FORTY-ONE

"I didn't know you had siblings," I say after an eternity, my voice rough.

"No one knows. It's not public information and has always been kept secret," the Marquis clears his throat and adjusts his tie. "My mother had an affair. Roman is the result of it."

Nothing seems to faze Roman. "You couldn't have described me any better," he says, patting the Marquis on the shoulder in an almost friendly manner.. "I've missed you."

The melody of strings drifts in from outside. My lips tremble, desperately searching for the right words, but my mind is blank.

"Compliment." Roman's gaze pierces into mine. Something about his presence unsettles me. His voice sounds beautiful, but it's too cold. Heartless. "He has never told anyone about me. You've cracked him."

My cheeks grow hot. Reflexively, I look to the Marquis, but he avoids my gaze and looks suspiciously focused on his pocket watch.

The same high cheekbones, the same dark blonde hair, and an aura of deadly arrogance.

"I can tell you're related."

"Can you?" Roman begins to approach me, lurking. His steps are calm and calculated.

"You share the same features." I step backward and

bump into the wall as he comes closer.

"Siblings share many things, Louise." The velvet of his voice envelops me, pressing on my chest, capturing every rational thought. "Memories, desires, dreams." He stops close in front of me. His long fingers start playing with a strand of hair that has come loose from my updo. "Toys."

"Enough." The Marquis' voice breaks through my trance. Roman has crossed an invisible line. His brother grabs him by the neck, pushes him forward, and smashes his forehead against the wall.

Something cracks.

I scream.

The Marquis lets him go.

Roman's face is covered in blood and he... laughs? "I knew it." Despite his split lip, he still looks enchanting. Not enchanting like the Marquis, not so unshakeable and strong, but mischievous and reckless. "She means something to you."

The Marquis does him the favor of not responding. An invisible fist clenches my stomach.

He tested him, provoked him, played with me to see how his brother would react.

I know that the Marquis does not tolerate men's hands on me that are not his, but I never really understood what it meant. I had assumed it was due to his vanity, the fact that he always wants to embody a perfect image outwardly. But his brother's words...

I clear my throat. "Arrogance runs in the family then. Good to know."

Roman laughs. "I like her. She's cheeky. I like that."

The darkness in the Marquis' eyes makes him shut up.

"Can we get back to our actual topic now?"

Roman nods. "Of course." He suddenly becomes deadly serious. "I can't stay much longer anyway. Although I wouldn't say I'm afraid of him, I don't want to push my luck. The quicker I get away, the better."

"Afraid of who?" I blurt out.

The Marquis's hand makes a dismissive gesture, telling me to keep quiet, but Roman is quicker. "My father. I'm hiding from him and he's here tonight."

"Roman..." growls the Marquis, but he continues speaking.

"I tried to kill him, but it didn't go as planned and now... the life of the only person who means something to me is at stake," says Roman.

The Marquis slaps him on the back of the head with his flat hand. "Are you out of your mind? Why are you telling her this?"

"I'm old enough, I can handle it," I say firmly, taking a step forward.

"But you have a loose tongue," he interrupts me, then looks back at Roman. "She will tell her sister about it."

Roman shrugs. "Whatever. That's not why I'm here. My sad story doesn't interest anyone. I came here, Jerome, to warn you. I have information that might interest you."

He throws me a furtive glance that doesn't escape my notice. "It's about the Circle. About Gino."

Gino. The name pierces my soul like a dagger. I've suppressed the sound of those four letters for too long, and now it feels like I'm learning about my family's fate for the first time. That's what happens when you run away from your demons instead of facing them head-on.

The Marquis heads towards the door. "Louise, you will leave us now."

"No!" I protest and step behind Roman. "I'm staying. If it's about Gino, it concerns me too."

Roman's shoulders shake as he suppresses another laugh. "I can only marvel. Someone standing up to the Marquis, what a sight to behold."

"Quiet. Both of you," my husband's tone is so firm that I hold my breath. "I'll give you five seconds, then you're out of this room."

The courage in me protests, but the fear is stronger - and I am a coward. I leave.

FORTY-TWO

Since I don't know where to go, because I don't know anyone in this ocean of wealthy faces, I return to the royal box.

If Charlotte were with me now, or Gabriel, we would puzzle together about all the possible secrets the Marquis is discussing with his brother at this moment, but the red velvet chairs next to me are empty and I am left alone with all my questions.

Bored, I play with the silk ribbon tied around my neck. Time passes slowly and when I hear footsteps approaching my box, my eyelids are heavy. I have to force myself not to fall asleep. The constant 3/4 time of the waltz makes me tired.

A click. The door opens behind me. The Marquis steps beside me. He appears calm, relaxed, but the throbbing vein on his neck betrays him.

"Finished?" I ask, yawning. "Can we go home?"

He smirks and sits on the chair right next to me. His leg touches mine. "You said home."

"Don't read too much into it."

The song ends, a new waltz begins. For a while, we silently watch the dancing couples below us.

"Would you like to dance?" he asks eventually.

"I would like to know what Gino is planning. I would like to know how much time I have left with Charlotte."

At the sound of her name, his face hardens.

"You are always curious, but you fail to realize one thing: we are not always capable of bearing the weight of the truths we chase after. Sometimes they crush us under their weight, and once they are set free, there is no turning back."

I don't return his gaze, instead, I study the gold stucco and ceiling painting of the hall intently.

"There are many truths that I keep hidden from you. Because your heart would break at them."

That's my cue. "Isn't that exactly what you intend? To see my little foolish heart break?"

His soft lips turn into a hard, dismissive line.

"You said it yourself. That you will leave me to my fate."

"You wouldn't understand." His Adam's apple twitches. It looks like he's choking on all the secrets he's forced to hide within himself. "It's better for you if you hate me."

The heat burning from his leg through the thin fabric of my dress finds its way between my thighs.

"Shouldn't I be allowed to decide for myself what danger is worth risking my soul for?"

He smirks. "Probably."

The silence between us is charged - it no longer remains still, but wordlessly whispers all the unspoken things we can't say to each other.

"What's more important to you, Louise? Your soul or your heart?"

From a distance, I see Madison making her way

through the crowd. She's obviously looking for her kavalier, the Marquis.

"I care about you," I whisper silently, so silently, but he hears me and his fingertips gently touch my thigh.

"It's important to me that you're safe, that you are well - and I'm ashamed of it because you have always been cold and dismissive towards me. Because you told me yourself that you feel nothing for me."

I take a deep breath. "But when you walk beside me, I feel safe. When I imagine you sleeping in the room next to mine, my nightmares vanish into thin air. When you were gone, for months, and I didn't know when or if I would see you again…I have never missed a person as much as I missed you. It feels like you're the missing piece that completes my soul."

I exhale deeply. I've carried these words with me for so long that they merged with me, until I've become accustomed to their weight. But now, as they leave my lips, I feel as light as I did before the wedding.

He's about to tell me that he's ashamed of me, of my naivety, my careless heart, my dreams that are too big for my small body.

When he remains silent after ten breaths that I count, hope creeps into my heart.

Maybe maybe. Maybe he feels the same and is mentally preparing to confess to me.

A clearing of his throat. He pushes his chair back.

"Excuse me, please," his cold voice cuts through

my heart and splits it in two. "There are still a few business partners waiting for me, with whom I have important matters to discuss. Our car is ready downstairs. The driver will take you home. I will see you tomorrow."

The sound of the closing door is my downfall. I want to die, from shame and regret.

Why didn't I just bite off my tongue instead of losing face in front of the one person who now knows he can mortally wound me?

FORTY-THREE

"What can I say? He's a jerk. We already knew that." Charlotte's voice sounds snappy and dismissive. She's still deeply hurt by the Marquis' behavior towards her, by the fact that he forbids her from entering the castle.

However, he didn't mention anything about phone calls. My feet dangle in the air as I lie on my stomach, talking to my sister, resting my head on my elbows and gazing at the gardens. I have come to love my bedroom by now.

"I practically confessed my love to him, Charlotte. This is serious. It's the biggest embarrassment possible. I can't just dismiss it by telling myself that he's a jerk. I know he is and yet I fell in love with him."

"Pathetic." Her brief responses tell me she doesn't want to talk about him anymore.

"Was it that bad? How he... treated you before I surprised you?"

"Bad?" Her voice rises two octaves. "Bad doesn't even begin to cover it. You saw how he grabbed me and pressed me against that shelf."

"How did it happen ?".

"Does that matter?"

"No. Yes. It doesn't change the fact that it was bad of him. Nothing justifies treating you like that. But

I'm still interested in why he suddenly decides, seemingly out of the blue, that we shouldn't have contact."

She snorts.

"That doesn't mean I doubt you. But if I understand where his anger comes from, then I can better convince him to let you into the house again."

"He won't."

She sounds determined, dangerously determined. The Charlotte I know is an optimist. She always believes that things can work out for the better and she never gives up without a fight.

"We'll find a way. In any case, things cannot continue as they are now. I'm not allowed to leave the property without him and you cannot visit me here. This cannot be a permanent situation."

"Louise..."

"I know there's a solution, it just has to…".

"Louise! He tried to kiss me."

FORTY-FOUR

My life is a mess. A pile of rubble that I desperately try to put in order, but the destruction is so overwhelming that I don't know where to start and find myself paralyzed in front of the shards of my dreams.

Gino is about to kill my mother and sister. It won't be long now. I'm married to a man who has nothing but indifference for me, and not only was I stupid enough to lose my heart to him, I was also tempted to confess it to him.

My thoughts are racing, turning into pure pain and pounding against the top of my skull from the inside, demanding to be released, but as much as I want to, I can't release the disappointment and hurt from my heart.

He tried to kiss her.

He tried to kiss my sister.

Charlotte.

Charlotte, whom he was supposed to save.

Maybe that was his idea of salvation. Maybe that was the plan all along. Maybe he's tired of me and regrets taking the wrong sister as his wife, not saving her life instead of mine.

I strain over every moment the three of us were in the same room. There aren't many of them and not a single memory flashes in my mind, not even a repressed one, that could give me a clue that the Marquis has feelings for my sister.

He wanted to kiss her.

When he kissed me, did he imagine it was her lips?

I'm so sorry for Charlotte. My heart aches to think of the fear she must have endured as his strong body pressed against her petite one and she had no way of knowing I would interrupt whatever he was doing.

How far would he have gone?

What would he have been willing to risk?

There's a soft knock on my door. I snap out of my thoughts. How much time has passed since I ended the phone call with Charlotte? Night has now fallen over me. Darkness fills the room because I didn't have the energy to turn on any of the lamps.

"Come in," my mouth answers for me. It's like I'm controlled by someone else.

His scent reaches my heart even before I see him.

"Get out," I say. He ignores it, but doesn't come any closer, instead standing as a dark shadow in the doorway.

"I've come to talk about what you confessed to me last night."

My heart clenches painfully. Nothing interests me more than what is on the tip of his tongue. I didn't sleep the whole of last night, restlessly tossing myself from side to side because I couldn't imagine anything other than what was going on in his inscrutable head.

But I can't. I can't even look at him without feeling

sick, let alone talk about feelings that no longer have any value, that have withered in my chest and taste like ash on my tongue.

"I don't want to hear it."

"Louise."

"I want you to leave me alone. I've already told you to only speak to me when it's absolutely necessary."

"Right after you confessed your love to me."

My vision goes black. My hands ball into fists. "Is it so difficult to give me the space I need? Do you really always have to disregard the needs of those around you? How can you be so cocky?"

He laughs. He really has the cheek to laugh. "If you're offended because I didn't answer right away…".

I jump up. My anger gets the best of me. "We're not talking about my damn pride or the lies I told you about my supposed love." My voice is louder than intended and the Marquis backs away from my anger. "I take back everything I said. I hate you!"

For a painful second I can read on his face what he really feels. That I'm ramming a dagger right into his heart and he's come to confess to me what I was longingly hoping for just a few hours ago. But now everything is different. Everything is ugly and cold.

"You tried to kiss Charlotte."

His mouth remains open.

"It's not enough that you allow another woman to live here with us, that you fuck her while I sleep just a few rooms away. No, that's not enough. You have to try it with my own sister, the one person who means more to me than anything else in the world?"

He is a proven fighter. He immediately composes himself and steps towards me.

"That's a lie". He emphasizes each word slowly and clearly. "Whatever she told you, it's made up."

His denial increases my anger tenfold. I'm on fire, ready to drag him with me into the pit of hell.

"You're a dog. You don't even have the decency to own up to your actions."

He bares his teeth. The thought of hell doesn't scare him. He was born there.

"I can overlook a lot and endure a lot," he growls from the depths of his lost soul. "But if there's one thing I hate, it's false accusations."

He gets closer and closer to me until I feel his breath on my face. "And I detest even more those who believe these lies, without evidence, without the courage to use their own minds and think for themselves."

It hurts me how beautiful he is. And I'm dying because I want to kiss him, even at this moment when I feel nothing for him but fear and anger.

"Next time you're about to tell me about your petty, childish emotions," he whispers, his lips close to my ear, "then swallow your words or choke on them for all I care, but don't bother me with them anymore."

I blink away the tears and when I open my eyes

again, he's already halfway out the door.

"I could never love you, Louise. Prepare for a cold rest of your life. That's the price you pay when you take a Marquis as your husband."

FORTY-FIVE
The Marquis

Every step takes me ten times as much energy as it does on normal nights. Nothing is normal anymore, not since she came into my life.

This all has to end.

The pain in my chest must die.

I wasn't made to feel. I wasn't raised to put other people's feelings before my own.

I'm a hypocrite. I spat in her face how much I despise liars, when I myself have spun my own fate out of untruths.

When I'm out of earshot, in the dark hall of mirrors reflecting the moonlight from outside, I stop.

Three deep breaths. A look at the mirrored walls. I am the Marquis. Nothing fazes me. Nobody trips me up.

I dial his number with steady fingers. He answers immediately.

"Gino. Regarding our agreement - it's only been nine months, but you can have her sooner. I've grown tired of her. Louise is yours. Kill her on Sunday."

MONDAY

The news of my mother's death reaches me at dinner. Suddenly the dessert tastes like tears. Three letters written in ink on a golden tray that Rousel carries into the room.

The Marquis reads the card first before handing it to me without a word.

Mother is dead.

Something in me hoped that Gino would spare her. Part of me believed that saying goodbye would be easier, now that I've already lost my father and my heart should be used to the feeling of death.

But the ground opens up beneath me and swallows me. All color disappears from my life.

My mother was never an anchor, never a refuge where I felt safe. She drank too much, expected too much, and never gave us enough of what we really needed, instead of expensive clothes and trips to luxury resorts: an honest kiss on the cheek, a warm hug, and the promise that she loves us no matter what we achieve in life.

She wasn't a saint. She had her flaws, her dark spots, but she was my mother. She was the person who knew me like no other and with whom I shared a part of my soul. That part is now gone. Her death has ripped it out of my chest. When I breathe, I feel the hole.

The Marquis signals to the staff with a brief gesture that they should leave the room. What he has to say is intended for my ears only.

"Should I find out for you how she died?"

I shake my head. "I don't know. I don't know if I want to know. Whether it would make things better or worse."

He pushes his chair back and approaches me, reaching for the back of the chair right next to me and sits down.

His warm hand rests on my cold one. I want to pull away, but I'm paralyzed. Faced with this loss, everything else fades into the background. I try hard to summon the feeling of anger towards my husband, but I'm empty.

For a while, we sit in silence together. He watches me, and I stare at my empty plate. White tulips on the table. One of them starts to wither, its head slowly succumbing to gravity.

Everything must pass.

"I will organize the funeral. You don't have to worry about anything," he says gently.

My body collapses. All strength leaves my bones.

"Let's go upstairs, to your room. You need rest now."

When I still don't move, he rises decisively, wraps his unyielding arms around me and presses me against his hard chest.

The castle is in darkness, only a few candles

burning in the corridors.

He holds onto me and carries me upstairs to my rooms. No one dares to speak to us, the staff turning into shadows, and no sign of Madison.

The Marquis gently lays me on my bed. I curl up into a ball, a helpless trembling ball, and clutch my legs.

"It hurts so much," I whisper breathlessly. "It feels like someone is slashing me from the inside."

"I know," he replies softly. His hand begins to stroke my hair. "It will pass. Not tomorrow, not the day after, but with time, the pain will become bearable. It will always be a part of you, but you will learn to live with it, instead of just surviving."

I struggle to sit up. His features appear so strong, so determined in the moonlight that I almost believe he could take all the pain away from me if I just ask him to.

"Why are you being so kind to me? After what I said to you yesterday?"

"That your feelings for me were just an act?"

"Yes…"

"Because I know that's not true. Your eyes give you away."

It almost feels wrong to talk about such trivial things on the day of my mother's death. I bite my lip.

"And because I know all too well what it feels like to be consumed by grief. I know the feeling of losing a loved one and being alone with the pain. No one should grieve alone. It changes you."

My questioning look prompts him to continue.

"The day I had to shoot my own father in the forehead was the darkest day of my life. I don't like to admit it, especially not to myself. It's easier to pretend that I enjoyed his death. But in reality, I miss him, and as much as I tell myself that he wanted it, that it was his task for me to pull the trigger, it doesn't free me from my guilt. My father's blood sticks to my hands."

Without thinking, I reach for his hand. Our fingers intertwine, his thumb gently stroking the back of my hand.

"May I tell you what I intended to say to you yesterday?" he asks cautiously. I don't know this soft side of him. He's like a different person.

I wonder if he has dropped his merciless mask for my sake or if he's deceiving me in this moment and playing a role. With him, everything is so unpredictable, so intricate and gray.

"Say it."

"You don't suffer from nightmares when you sleep near me, because you know that I will protect you everywhere - in this world and in any other, even if it's just a dream," he says, stroking my hair again. "You are the most precious thing I have ever held in my hands - and that means a lot."

A sigh escapes my chest. Although my body is still made entirely of pain, his voice eases my suffering a little. Without needing to say a word, I move away from him, making space for him on the mattress, and he understands.

Silently, he lies down by my side. His arms wrap around my body. His warmth seeps into every cold corner.

He hugs me from behind and I hold onto my legs. He kisses my neck. Finally, I manage to cry. I sob until dawn - and the Marquis doesn't release his grip for a second. When the first rays of sun tickle my face, I slowly doze off. When I open my eyes again, he is gone.

TUESDAY

He is waiting for me in the small dining room with breakfast. He's laid out a lavish spread as if there's something to celebrate, but the sight of all the food makes my stomach clench.

Tiered trays full of fruit, pastries, salmon, caviar smile at me. The Marquis's plate is still empty.

He looks at me. "Sit down."

"I can't eat anything."

"You must. You'll only feel worse if you starve yourself."

Because his tone sounds strict and I lack the strength to argue after the restless night, I follow his command.

Lola pours me coffee. The steam envelops my face in a fragrant cloud.

"Were you able to sleep a little?" He spears a bunch of grapes onto a long, narrow gold fork. "I wanted to let you rest a little, that's why I left."

He apologizes for leaving my room? These are entirely new tones.

"Please eat." With his elegant fingers, he gestures to my empty plate. When I still don't react, he gets up, takes my plate and begins to fill it with what he knows I like. Strawberries, sugared cream, mini croissants, and butter.

Gently, he places the plate in front of me. He has arranged the food beautifully.

"Thank you," I say softly.

"She speaks." His smile is genuine. Where is the Marquis I know? The angry one who seeks revenge on the world, for all the wounds he has mostly inflicted on himself? In front of me sits a man, whom one could almost believe to be a loving husband.

"If you eat half of the plate, you can ask me a question, no matter what it is, and I will answer honestly."

He already knows me too well. He knows how curious I am, how much I love to get to the bottom of secrets that are not meant for me.

"And if I finish the whole thing?"

"Then you get three questions."

I don't want to smile. It feels so wrong, on the day after my mother's death, but I can't stop my mouth as a warm feeling runs through my body.

The Marquis reveals to me a tender, caring side of himself that no one else knows. *Except for Madison,* something whispers inside me, but I silence the voice with a determined bite into my croissant.

Satisfied, the Marquis leans back, sips his coffee, and watches me. I dip the tip of the croissant into my cup, watching as the pastry slowly soaks up the liquid.

"One of my ancestors brought croissants to Marie Antoinette's court." It's obvious that he wants to distract me, to take my mind off things - and I'm grateful for it.

"Marie Antoinette has always fascinated me," I say

softly.

"I know." He reaches into the inner pocket of his jacket and pulls out the fountain pen I gave him on my first visit.

"You carry it with you?"

"Of course. Even though I probably shouldn't, given its age. Any collector would probably behead me for it. But I like to carry it with me. Every time I have to write something, it reminds me of you."

A grape bursts between my teeth. "My plate is half empty. Can I ask the first question?"

He nods.

I don't even have to think about what I want to know from him, but only have to decide which of the questions on my endless imaginary list I will prioritize. "Why did you offer to marry me to my parents?"

He takes the napkin from his lap and dabs his mouth with it. The situation in which he doesn't embody pure elegance has yet to be brought to life.

"My answer will not please you: I don't know."

Disappointed, I slump back in my chair. He wins every game.

"Do you want me to explain it to you?"

I nod.

"I was never particularly close to your family. Yes, it's true that our grandfathers were friends and both members of the Circle, which makes them almost like brothers. But I myself never had much to do with your father. He was always more of a lone wolf."

I can't disagree with him. My father's selfish stubbornness has brought us all to ruin and let his bloodline die out.

"When I heard from Gino that you were on his list, I didn't care. I had no connection to you, and I've seen too many people die for one more or less to make a difference to me."

I feel cold. I will never get used to death being a part of our families' everyday lives.

"Then I saw you at the debutante ball. You were too nervous to notice me. I didn't try to approach you, but just stood on the edge of the dance floor as you came down the stairs with your kavalier, and thought to myself, *what a waste of beauty if she were to die.* Without ulterior motives. I had no intention of getting physically close to you or stealing your heart. All I knew was that I didn't want you to die."

"Even though Madison is your partner?"

His eyes narrow. His tender angry eyes.

"Madison and I stayed together out of habit. We haven't been happy for a long time."

"Haven't been?"

"I ended the relationship."

"Because of me?"

He looks up at me. "You've used up your question."

Obediently, I take another bite of the croissant and dip a strawberry in cream. We eat in silence.

Some days I get the feeling that time passes differently in the Marquis' house, sometimes slowly, sometimes much too quickly, and never in the way that I need it to.

I wash down the last bite with coffee. "Don't you have any questions for me?", I ask. My face burns with excitement.

At times, we're so close to each other, and two breaths later, it feels as if I'm seeing him for the first time in my life.

"Many, actually. But I don't want to make you blush. Most of these are not meant to be spoken out loud in daylight. I will whisper them in your ear at the right moment."

My shoulders tense up. He means it. He lowers his head and looks at me intently.

"Are you trying to take advantage of my mental state to get me to sleep with you?", I whisper.

"Is that your second question?"

"No. I'm saving it."

He nods. "Then let's go. There's something I want to show you."

A NOBLE CONTRACT

STILL TUESDAY
The Marquis

At the age of six, I started learning fencing. At ten, an opponent slashed my cheek in a duel. A barely visible scar runs across my left cheekbone.

When I'm nervous, it tingles. I haven't felt it for years, but as I lead Louise into the stables ahead of me, I instinctively run my hand over it, as if the touch could dispel the pain.

The scar stings. It reminds me that I am a sinner.

Louise is so delicate. So fragile under my large hands. Her soft hair blows in the wind as she stops and turns hesitantly to me. "Where are we going?" She detects something in my gaze that unsettles her.

"You'll see when we get there." At first, I felt flattered by her trust, but now it gnaws at me. The last human part of me that has survived all these years of deceit and cold-bloodedness wants to believe that we both have a chance at a happy life. A life together. That I can kiss her without dragging her into ruin with me.

But life is not a fairy tale - and villains don't get happy endings.

Louise

All I can think about are the two questions I am still allowed to ask him.

There is so much I want to know. About his childhood, his youth, the future he plans, and the dark rooms where he locks away the secrets of his past.

Ombre's snort brings me back to reality. He's already saddled up. I turn to the Marquis. "Where are we going?"

Pain flickers in his eyes. Another secret that I will never uncover. "You'll see when we get there."

Without further discussion, I give in. Normally, I don't like surprises, but I am also smart enough to know when it's pointless to push the Marquis. He speaks when he deems the time right.

He places a hand on the small of my back.

"You don't plan to go riding, do you?" The panic in my voice is evident.

"You've already overcome your fear once. What's stopping you from doing it again?"

I protest, planting my hands on my hips. "Involuntarily, if I may remind you. You put me on Ombre's back without asking. I almost had a heart attack. You should be glad I'm still standing alive in front of you."

He laughs. Not suppressed, not dry - but from the depths of his chest, from his whole soul. A genuine laughter like I've never heard before.

My first reaction is to punch him in the stomach.

"Ouch!" I scream as my knuckles hit the hard muscles under his suit. "Damn it!"

Deep down, I know that I'm not really angry, but just looking for an excuse to touch him. The sharp pain in my hand is the punishment for it.

He still smiles as he takes my fingers in his and checks them for injuries. "You're fine," he chuckles and holds onto me a breath too long.

Good. I'm not the only one who is magnetically drawn to him and has to fight every second not to throw myself around his neck.

His white teeth gleam. I wonder how their bite would feel around my nipples.

"You're drooling," he says dryly, and he's back to his old self, cool and reserved.

To hide my embarrassed face from him, I quickly turn to Ombre. "Why are you so obsessed with seeing me ride?"

"Because it's one of my favorite positions," he replies so dryly that I initially think I misheard and choke on my saliva out of nervousness. I'm overwhelmed by a coughing fit, and he pats me on the back.

"We ride together, then it's easier to find the right rhythm," he says, and his voice doesn't reveal whether he's serious or teasing me.

"Okay, stop, that's enough." I raise both hands protectively in front of me and turn to face him. "If this is going to work at all, you need to stop making innuendos."

"If what exactly is supposed to work?" he asks, his voice suddenly deeper. He steps closer to me.

Without thinking, I put one foot in the stirrup, grab Ombre's neck, and swing myself onto his back. The Marquis looks up at me. His eyes flash devilishly. It dawns on me...

"You did that on purpose! You distracted me again."

He tilts his head. "When you think about things unrelated to your fear, it's easier to defy it."

And he swings up behind me.

He's everywhere. His warm breath tickles my ear. His hard chest presses against my back, his muscular arms wrap around my shoulders, his beautiful fingers rest in my lap holding the reins.

But the center of my attention, the one thing that makes my heart race ahead before the horse beneath us even moves, are his spread legs behind mine, his most secret place against my backside.

I can feel him - and I know immediately that he would definitely be too big for me.

"Nervous?" he whispers in my ear from behind.

"Not in the slightest," I lie, and he clicks his tongue. Ombre starts to run.

The Marquis's castle is not far from Versailles. Although it is smaller, the estate does not lack in attention to detail and grandeur compared to its model.

A hidden part of the gardens has not yet been revealed to me. I know the mazes, the fountains, and seas of flowers, tulips, roses, hyacinths, the secret paths and intricately wrought gates, but I have no idea what awaits me today.

The Marquis urges Ombre on, and his castle becomes smaller in the distance. Riding was once my dream, then the thread from which my world was woven, and finally my greatest nightmare.

As the Marquis embraces me from behind, sets the pace, and we move in the same rhythm, there is no trace left of the old fear.

My throat is tight. I'm afraid of not being afraid by his side, because what happens if I fearlessly venture too far forward, into new strange dreams, and he is gone one day? Will I still be so brave or will I no longer find my way back home?

We reach a forest.

"I didn't know your estate was that large."

"There's a lot you don't know about me," he smiles and spurs Ombre on.

We gallop into the green thicket, past ancient firs and treetops bowing before the Marquis. Faster and faster, ever breathless.

"Lean forward," his voice flies past my ear. I bury my fingers deeper into Ombre's mane and rest on his warm neck.

We are one. We run in a race against time. The time that remains for us. His warm body presses against mine from behind. I want nothing more than to let go, to lean into his chest, I want him to kiss my neck and promise that he will love me.

He ducks as we ride under a thick branch and pulls me down with him.

He will be the end of me.

The forest begins to clear. The Marquis's cheek brushes mine, and I feel the touch of a growing beard.

Before us lies a paradise. I'm used to wealth. But it's not the splendor of the pavilion, whose dome appears behind one of the green hills, not the adjacent lake with swans and boats floating on it.

It's the feeling of pure silence and peace that shields this place from the rest of the world.

It's as if I'm looking at a painting, sinking into it, a hidden beauty that no one has seen before me. A retreat that the Marquis only shares with me.

"This is my sanctuary," he says, and I can hear in his voice that he understands my silence as admiration.

He's right.

On Ombre's back, we move over the thick, lush grass and finally come to a stop right in front of the gold-adorned pavilion.

The Marquis dismounts, then reaches out his hand to help me off the horse. His fingers burn into my hip.

"What kind of place is this?"

"My father had the pavilion built for my mother. As a wedding gift. He wanted a hideaway where they could always be undisturbed."

"It's beautiful."

The Colbert family crest is displayed above the rounded entrance door, a wolf baring its teeth behind curved letters. How fitting.

The Marquis doesn't tie Ombre up, but lets him run freely in the near paddock.

"Would you like to go inside?"

I look around. The beauty of nature surrounding us gets under my skin. The sunlight breaks on the small lake in precious gold. A field hare sprints past us. For the first time in months, I feel truly safe. At home.

"Yes," I whisper, and the Marquis pulls an antique key from his pocket.

"Do you always carry that with you?"

"Only on special days."

Today is a special day for him. He's spending it with me. Goosebumps shiver down my spine. I have to remind myself not to lose my head. All of this could be a game for him, a trivial pastime. Only God knows - or the devil - what plan he's pursuing.

The key opens the door to his hideaway. The pavilion is not large, and I love it at first sight. Inside, I feel as if time has stood still for three hundred years. It seems as if nothing has been touched or changed since Marie Antoinette's downfall.

Pale pink silk, paintings and candles, floor-to-ceiling windows, velvet curtains, a floor of black and white stone. A fireplace with a fire already burning in it.

My gaze lingers on the bed in the back of the room. "Do you sometimes sleep here?"

The Marquis closes the door behind us. The clicking sound has a finality to it. "Rarely. When I need to clear my head and don't want anyone to find me. Then I spend the nights here."

How I wish I knew how many women he has brought here before. "And what are we doing here?"

"Whatever you wish. I wanted to show you this place because I thought you might like it. No expectations. We will do whatever you feel like."

He goes to the fireplace and throws a log into the fire, then reaches for the poker and begins to poke at the flames.

"I think I would like to rest a little." The death of my mother weighs heavy on me, and my gut feeling tells me that I will never be the same again.

Tired, I let myself fall onto the edge of the bed.

The Marquis has turned his back to me. "Do you want to be alone?" he asks.

The thought of being surrounded by silence and having to confront my inner demons is unbearable.

"Please stay," I reply softly.

The eyes of his ancestors, captured in oil paintings, watch me, their curious gaze piercing under my skin.

The resemblance that runs through the Colbert bloodline makes me shudder. They are all a bit too intense, too demanding, too destructive.

"Is your brother still in the country?" It's the first thing that comes to mind to break the uncomfortable silence.

He tilts his head. His gaze is inscrutable. "I didn't bring you here to talk about other men," he says, running his hand through his hair.

He doesn't realize that every one of his movements is perfect.

Before I know it, he's kneeling close in front of me, between my legs, holding my hand. He's so tall that we're almost the same height, even though he's on his knees. "You are here because I want to show you that I will always find places where you're safe, no matter what happens. As long as you're married to me, I will take care of everything you need - and right now, that's peace and a hiding place from the world that has hurt you so deeply."

I don't want to cry. I want to show him the strong fighter that I am on good days - but all the bad ones have accumulated inside me, and as his thumb strokes over the back of my hand, the pain breaks free.

Two warm drops travel down my cheek. I've long run out of tears. He wipes them from my face with his fingertips. "Everything will be okay, Louise. I promise."

For the duration of two lifetimes and a breath, we look into each other's eyes. I lose myself in him. Before I could begin to believe that we are about to kiss, before I can move my face closer to him, he forces himself to wake up from this dream, closes his eyes briefly, takes a deep breath, and gathers himself.

As if he wants to remind himself that he has a mission.

He stands up. "Behind this door," - he points next to the fireplace - "is a bathroom. In case you want to freshen up. I still have some phone calls to make and will take a walk in the woods for that. Think about what you want for dinner."

I've tried to unsettle the Marquis in countless ways, but I never thought that I would succeed with a burger and fries.

With a puzzled expression, he looks at the order that has just arrived. He's so accustomed to his private chefs that it completely throws him off guard that I ordered fast food through an app.

"How did the delivery guy even find us here?" he asks in a sour tone.

"And I thought you were the smart one of the two of us. Do you know what GPS is?"

His smile is dark. "I will have to kill him. No one besides you knows about this place and it should stay that way."

I almost choke on my fries. The young driver's friendly face flickers in my mind's eye and I feel sick. "You wouldn't dare."

He waves it off with a laugh. I still have to get used to his laughter. "It's just too tempting to tease you," he says as he sits down next to me on the bed and nudges my chin with his index finger.

"You would believe anything I say, wouldn't you?"

My discomfort doesn't dissipate; in fact, it grows.

"Is this all a game to you?" I ask, focusing on reading every movement of his face, every seemingly insignificant twitch.

Nothing. His expression doesn't change even a little bit.

"I like to play. But not with feelings. At least not with yours," he replies, and it sounds sincere. I take a deep breath. His scent is intoxicating.

"Do you feel like playing, Louise?"

His entire demeanor changes, transforming into something dark and unfathomable. His tone sounds possessive as he says, "What games do you know?"

My neck burns. I swallow. "I want to ask my second question," it shoots out of me.

The Marquis lingers in his predatory stance for a moment, then his shoulders relax and he smiles a sugary-sweet half-smile that makes him look ten years younger. "Go ahead," he says expectantly, looking at me.

"Are you planning to ever give away your heart and fall sincerely in love?"

Silence. The darkness of the night presses against the windows from outside. Our breath fogs up the glass. The fire crackles in the fireplace. His gaze becomes more honest, more vulnerable.

"No," he says curtly, and I am too deeply affected to ask further.

At least he admits it. A branch hits the window from outside. I flinch. The Marquis places both hands on my shoulders.

"You are too trusting. I mean it. Don't give away your heart so easily." His hands wander along my neck, to my face, and rest on my glowing cheeks.

The gesture whispers something so deeply familiar that it feels as if we know each other from a previous life.

"You are too reckless, Louise. You trust people whose facade you cannot see through."

I want to turn my face away, but his grip is firm and determined, and he doesn't let go. "No one would ever know if something happened to you here. No one would know where to look for you."

He's making me uneasy.

"I may be naive," I blurt out. It hurts to hold his gaze. "But you're a coward."

He lets go of me.

"You think hiding behind your walls of ice makes you stronger. But you're alone - and will always be alone. It's eating you up. I can see it in your eyes."

He's not used to hearing the truth.

"What do you really want from me, Louise?" he asks, his voice a dark shadow.

"I want you to make me your wife. Truly make me your wife. With everything that comes with it." I press my thighs together harder. I can't believe I've finally said it out loud.

Silently, he begins to tidy up the packaging of my food delivery, crumpling the paper and standing up to throw the trash in the bin.

He then paces back and forth in the small pavilion, seeming restless, contemplative. Finally, he abruptly stops.

"Do you even know what that means?" He looms over me like a proud, powerful king, on the verge of pronouncing my death sentence. "Do you have any idea of the magnitude it would have if I were to grant your wish?"

He adjusts his collar, a gesture that seems almost nervous. "Can you imagine what it could cost you to be my wife?"

To be honest, I've never really thought the thought through. Instead, I've only ever imagined the beginning of our story, the first moments, but never what would follow after.

A life with him. A real life with him - what would that look like?

I only know fragments of him. A shared dinner. An obligatory visit to a ball. A chance encounter in the hallway. What is he willing to give if he truly opens up?

"Look at me when I'm talking to you. Let me see your pretty face, darling."

We are so far away from everything. If I scream, no one will hear me. I'm at his mercy.

He grabs my chin.

"Look at me, I said."

I obey.

"If I make you my wife, you belong to me. With every cell of your body. You laugh for me, you breathe for me, you only have eyes for me, and you only fuck me. Do you understand?"

I nod.

"Every thought of yours belongs to me, every dream you dream, every desire you feel. You belong to me. Do you really want that?"

I swallow.

I shouldn't want it.

I shouldn't lose my innocence.

"Yes. I want it."

He growls and curls his lips in a way that almost looks like he's disgusted. Or aroused. I can't tell.

He turns around and shows me his back again, slowly walking towards the fireplace where the warming fire flickers.

He pokes the embers.

"Undress."

I catch my breath. "Excuse me?"

"Undress."

All warmth has left his voice, all tenderness. Before me stands the Marquis I know, hands braced on the edge of the fireplace, slightly bent forward. He stares transfixed into the flames, as if they could answer a question for him, one I don't know how to ask.

This moment is a déjà vu. It reminds me of our wedding night, during which he forced me to undress and then left me untouched.

So much has happened since then.

So much time has passed.

His words echo within me.

He will never give me his heart.

He will never be ready to love me.

But he is ready to make me his wife. Whatever that means...

Slowly, I unbutton my blouse. One button at a time. With every inch of bare skin touched by the cool night air, I make myself more vulnerable. The blouse falls to the ground, followed by my pants, my socks.

Finally, I stand there only in my underwear, in moon light and flickering candles.

The Marquis still has his back turned to me. "Underwear."

He knows me too well. I hesitate. I shouldn't do this. I will lose myself in him. On the other hand... what do I have left to lose now? One night. Just one night and I will finally know what it feels like to be possessed by a man. My bra falls. My panties.

He turns around, looks at the small pile of lace on the floor.

"You wear such underwear?" A devilish grin. "And I thought you were a good girl. Look how deceived one can be."

One look at his perfectly tailored trousers, which are suddenly much too tight in one particular place, tells me that I'm not the only one who is almost burning up with arousal.

"Get on your knees".

I follow without objection.

"Lower your head. Look at the ground."

The cold stone floor burns my bare skin.

"That might hurt a little."

His leather shoes appear in my field of vision. He reaches for something. A metal clink fills the room.

The poker... Except it's not a poker.

Panic rises within me. No. He won't do that. He's just playing on my fears. He just wants to find out where my limits are. How far I'm willing to go.

He pulls the metal out of the fire. His dark silhouette looms in front of me. I dare not look up at him.

"You want to be my wife?" When I don't answer, he grabs my hair, burying his fingers in it, and jerks my head back so that I'm forced to meet his gaze. "Answer."

"Yes," I whisper. "I do." It's as if we're repeating the staged wedding in our own way, just for us alone. Without a priest. Without God. Just the handsome devil smiling at me.

"Then so be it. You are mine. Your heart, your soul, your body."

And he presses the glowing branding iron against my chest. Everything goes black.

Everything is spinning. Everything hurts. My entire existence has shrunk to the two centimeters of burnt skin. To the smell of burnt flesh.

I feel like throwing up. I quickly get up, run into the bathroom and retch until my stomach cramps and I can't breathe anymore.

The Marquis doesn't follow me. He waits in the dark.

After what feels like an eternity, I manage to get up from the cold marble floor. I wash my face with ice-cold water and look in the mirror above the sink. My scream gets stuck in my throat. "What have you done?"

My angry steps carry me towards him. I slam into his chest. He shows no reaction.

"What the hell have you done?" My fists drum on his chest, hitting him over and over again until he becomes bored, grabs my wrists, and shakes me.

"Louise!" His tone is so sharp that I immediately freeze. "I warned you. I'm not a man from your dreams. I'm everything you fear."

He lightly blows on the burnt spot on my chest to ease the pain. I shrink back.

"You belong to me now. This way, my dear, you will be reminded every day, no matter where you are or how many miles separate us." He winks at me. "You can get dressed again."

I can't believe it.

I've fallen for him.

Again.

The pain is unbearable. Inside me and on me. He has branded me. He has burned his initials into my chest.

I hope Gino will kill *him* instead of my sister.

Outside, behind the centuries-old windows, the wind howls and I wish it would carry me away, far away, where no one will ever remember me, to a warm place where the sun shines day and night and life kisses my wounds.

Meanwhile, the Marquis slips out of his shoes, takes off his jacket, and begins to unbutton his shirt. He prepares for sleep.

"No." My voice sounds strange. I'm no longer the girl I was just a few months ago. Too much has happened in too short a time.

"We are not going to sleep now. This night is not over yet."

I can't say what's driving me, whether it's the unsatisfied lust that's been building up inside me for weeks or the longing to win against the Marquis, to disarm him and dominate him. Whatever it is, it's stronger than me.

I grab him from behind. He whirls around to face me. And suddenly his lips are mine and my secrets are his.

We are one. The tips of our tongues meet in the middle, circling each other like hungry animals.

He grabs my hips. His fingers dig into my flesh. I gasp.

"Are you really sure you want this?" he asks in a hoarse voice. The vein on his neck throbs dangerously.

"I've never wanted anything more," I breathe.

His teeth sink into my neck. He bites me, gently touching my skin with the tip of his tongue, drawing circles on my lower back with his fingers.

He teases me, every touch a silent promise, a glimpse of everything he's capable of making me feel.

"Get on your knees."

I doubt my sanity as I comply with his request, despite what he did to me just a few minutes ago. He doesn't deserve the trust I give him, but my body is on fire, the pounding between my legs hinders my breathing, and of all the desires I ever held within me, only one has survived: to submit to the Marquis.

I sink to my knees. In this position, I have a perfect view of the hard bulge in his pants.

He takes a step back, walks over to the desk in the corner, opens a drawer, and I hold my breath, half expecting to see a knife or something similar in his hands with which he will hurt me.

But instead of gleaming metal, I discover delicate fabric caressing his fingers. A blindfold.

"Close your eyes," he says gently. The cool silk kisses my face, and when I open my eyes again, all I see is black night.

I'm so full of adrenaline, my senses are heightened like never before. I feel everything more intensely, smell my arousal, hear his breath close to my ear, even though he's towering above me, can feel the touch of his fingers, even though his hands don't brush me.

The buckle of a belt.

The zipper of his pants.

"Open your mouth".

I wish I could see him because I know he's

magnificent and impressive and I want to admire him.

He strokes my chin. I open my lips. The tip of his hard cock hits my teeth. He exhales loudly.

"You always have such a big mouth. Show me what it can do, other than insulting me."

I moan. Short and quiet, but he hears it and a small laugh escapes his throat.

He decisively grabs my hair. I take his dick between my lips.

"Yes, darling. That's exactly how I imagined it."

I've never blown a man before. It feels unusual and strange as he sinks into me, first hesitantly, then more determined and ever deeper. I gag. He pulls back.

I knew what to expect, I knew that his size would be overwhelming, but it's one thing to see the outline of its magnificence hidden beneath fabric and quite another to actually feel it on the back of my throat.

He's so big that I can't breathe and I haven't even taken it all in yet. How will it ever fit between my legs without tearing me apart?

His thumb strokes my cheek. Curious, I let the tip of my tongue slide over his shaft. It tastes like lonely nights when I masturbate while thinking about him.

I'm completely at his mercy, naked and blindfolded. Seconds pass and I slowly start to become more daring. Something inside me wants to find out how much it will take to make him explode.

My lips form a circle closing around his velvety,

warm skin. Back, forth, back and forth.

He groans.

"You're doing well, Louise. Very good." Goosebumps on my bare breasts. "I could almost think you've done this before."

I recognize the hidden question, see through the masked curiosity behind his words, and deny him the satisfaction of knowing whether he's the first man I've blowed. But the fact that he's asking fills me with a new sense of confidence. It means I'm doing my job well.

He pushes deeper into me. My gag reflex makes me shudder. My eyes are watering. It feels so good – finally being in control.

"Did you secretly dream about this?" he whispers and quickens his pace. "Is that what you wanted – to kneel naked in front of me and have your mouth fucked like a whore?"

The magic spot between my legs pulsates so hard that I almost think I'm going to cum without touching it.

I flinch as he rips the blindfold off my face. My hair is standing in all directions and my breathing is heavy.

His dick hovers just a few inches in front of me, majestic and proud, perfectly curved and beautiful. My spit makes it shine wet.

My knees ache. The cold stone burns into my skin, my bones.

The Marquis doesn't move. I look up at him

expectantly. He looks down at me with an intensity that makes all the walls I've built around me over weeks and months crumble to dust.

"Tell me, what you've secretly dreamed of? What did your fantasies look like?"

I return his gaze hungrily.

"Speak."

I press my lips tightly together. It's easy to dream of forbidden things, but when you speak them, they become real. Once my dark desires take shape, I could be crushed under their weight.

His thumb wanders between my lips. It's hard to imagine that this man, who touches me so tenderly, is capable of such destructive violence.

"I've imagined...". I close my eyes. I can't look at him while I confess. "...how you lean me over your desk and take me from behind. How you sink into me, thrust into me and can no longer control yourself because I'm the only one you want and who can satisfy your hunger."

"Go on."

"I've imagined that you leave Madison for me, that we meet in a secret room only known to us, and you kiss my neck, reach between my legs and whisper in my ear that you've never felt for anyone what you feel for me."

"Open your eyes."

I force myself to obey.

"Tell me honestly - if I weren't rich, not powerful and able to save your life - would you still feel the same? Would you wish to be touched by me if I could offer you nothing but my heart?"

My eyes still tear, but this time they burn not with desire, but with deep sadness. It seems so inconceivable to him that someone could love him for who he really is. Not the billions in the bank. Not the expensive cars and perfectly tailored suits - him. Not the Marquis, but Jerome.

"I would always love you," I say softly.

"And I would find you in every life," he replies. and then he rams into my throat, so deep that I gag, but he doesn't slow his pace, instead thrusting and thrusting and thrusting until his dick is bulging and his knees begin to shake.

I want to taste him, want him to cum in my mouth, but at the last second he pulls back, cups his dick with one hand and massages his tip.

He tilts his head back. He is a god. And he cums all over my face.

Warm thick semen flows down my face. A drop runs between my lips and I taste it on my tongue.

His breathing is only slowly returning to normal. He has his eyes closed, sweat on his forehead, and his blonde hair in wild strands across his beautiful face.

I struggle to get up from the stone floor. My knees are shaking with unbearable pain and my skin burns like fire. I collapse onto the edge of the bed.

He sits up.

"You can get dressed," he says so matter-of-factly, so unaffected, that one might think we had just finished a business meeting, not an intimate encounter.

"Are you serious?"

Without giving me another glance, he steps into the bathroom. I hear the sound of running water as he washes up.

Silent minutes pass. I feel cold, but I'm defiant and refuse to slip back into my clothes.

He came - while I'm still sick with pleasure. I can't take this any longer. He *has* to touch me or I'll lose my mind.

When he returns, he still doesn't look at me. I stand up and grab his wrist. My chest is heaving.

"Did you really just use me to blow you and now leave me behind like a used toy?"

He turns to stone. His profile could not have been carved more perfectly in stone by Michelangelo.

"Don't provoke me," he growls. "Don't ruin this perfect night."

I don't let go of his arm.

"Or are you afraid that you won't be able to satisfy me? Did I blow you so well that you're under pressure? Are you backing out because you know you can't make me come?"

One step too far. He bares his teeth, breaks free from my grip and brings his face close to mine.

"Believe me, if I were to fuck you, really fuck you, I would have to brand your name into your skin as well because you would forget it in the heat of the moment. This cheeky mouth," he grabs my chin and presses my lips into a pout, "would beg me not to stop and say everything I ever wanted to hear from you, just to be fucked for another round."

I want to hate him. But my body loves him. My skin tingles. My mouth is dry.

"Then make your threats real," I whisper. "Fuck me like you've never fucked anyone before. Let me forget my name."

When he doesn't respond, I shed my last bit of dignity and say softly, "Please."

He grimaces. Pain flashes behind his perfect mask. "If I did that, you would fall completely in love with me. If we sleep together, you will lose yourself in me and maybe never find yourself again. I won't do that to you."

"I am old enough to decide for myself who I fall in love with."

"But not scared enough of what I could do to you. You don't know me - and you don't want to admit that I would break your heart. Slowly and painfully." He kisses me fleetingly and quickly, almost lovingly. "Piece by piece."

Frustrated, I fall back onto the mattress and stare into space.

"I'm doing you a favor, believe me. Right now, you're convinced that you want me. Soon enough, you'll thank me for not giving in to your pleas." He lifts my chin. "You will soon hate me, Louise."

"I don't believe that."

He sighs. "You are too good for this world."

We don't speak a word all night and we don't touch each other once - but I can tell from his restless breathing that he, too, finds no sleep.

Our souls have become entwined. Now we must find a way to untangle ourselves from each other, because obviously the Marquis is not ready to truly open up to me despite everything I am willing to give.

WEDNESDAY

Even in the morning, we don't speak a word. We're both too stubborn to take the first step, so we ride back to the castle on Ombre in silence.

The Marquis helps me dismount, signals to one of the stable boys to unsaddle the horse, and then heads towards the back entrances.

I follow him.

We've silently dressed after waking up and ridden back immidiately.

My stomach grumbles, hoping that the staff has already set out breakfast.

As I step into the warm hallway, my heart becomes heavy again. Out in nature, so untouched by real life, it was easy for me to push away the death of my mother. Now, as I inhale the smell of the castle, everything comes flooding back. My hands start to tremble.

The Marquis doesn't notice my sudden change in mood; he's too busy checking his phone and pretending I don't exist.

We enter the dining room.

"Louise! There you are!"

The Marquis and I look up at the same time, but while my face begins to light up, his jaw twitches dangerously.

"Charlotte!" I exclaim, ignoring the fact that my

husband has banned her from the house. We embrace each other. Charlotte takes my face in both hands and scans me, letting her gaze wander over my body as if searching for injuries.

"Are you okay? I've been so worried about you," she says, pressing me to her chest once again.

"Has something happened?", I manage to ask, even though she's squeezing the air out of me. She releases the embrace.

"I arrived here last night because I wanted to check on you. It's been days since I last heard from you." I don't miss the suspicious look she throws at the Marquis. He deserves it.

"We went on a trip, sorry for not keeping in touch," I reply.

"It's okay." Her eyes become shiny, but she's not the type to cry in front of others. She fights her battles in secret, with herself. "Since Mother is no longer here... I'm scared, Louise. So terribly scared."

The presence of the Marquis presses down on my neck. I can feel him without looking at him, his tense posture, his menacing gaze.

"I don't want to interrupt your sisterly moment," he says, and Charlotte cuts him off. "But you are."

"You're banned from entering the house - and you know exactly why. Should I tell Louise what you did?"

A fight between the two is the last thing I need right now.

Charlotte takes a step towards him. "You can

whisper as many lies in her ear as you want, but she will always believe me. She's my sister and she knows that I only have the best intentions for her."

"Of course," he sniffs. Then he looks at me. "Do you want her to stay?"

I nod.

"Good," he says through clenched teeth. "You have ten minutes. If you're still here after that," - a menacing undertone in his voice - "I will personally drag you out the door."

His footsteps fade away in the hallway. We are alone.

"Bastard." Charlotte's face is no longer the one I know. Her youth, her confidence, the freshness of her soul have given way to a shadow that makes her look older. Lost.

"Don't take it to heart. You know how he is. He won't change."

She squints and looks into me. "You knew he tried to kiss me and still spent the night with him?"

I blush. "We didn't have sex, if that's what you're thinking." But we were very close - and the skin on my chest burns like hell, where the brand begins to heal. "He wanted to show me something to distract me from Mother's... death."

She tilts her head back and sighs. "You shouldn't trust him. I've tried to convince myself of his goodness for a long time, for your sake. I just wanted to hope that he's not as bad as his reputation. But doesn't it seem suspicious to you? That he starts getting close to you right now, takes you on a trip, when I start warning you? That he bans me and drives a wedge between us because I tell you the truth about what he did?"

My skin burns. My sweaty hands clench into fists.

He wanted to kiss her, he wanted to kiss her, he wanted to kiss her.

I'm so stupid.

Charlotte is right.

She confided in me, confessed what the Marquis tried to do to her, and instead of distancing myself from him, I allowed him to exploit my weakness, my grief, and manipulate me again.

Instead of punishing him for what he did, I gave in to him.

I hate myself.

Charlotte seems to guess my thoughts. She squeezes my hand. "You thought with your pussy, I would have done the same."

Completely taken aback, I choke on my own spit and have to laugh, even though it feels wrong. "You're the worst sister in the world."

"And you're the best, that's why you'll promise me to stay away from him. He's playing a game."

Her genuine concern moves me. She tucks a strand of hair behind my ear. "I know he looks good, that he's sexy and all... but that can't be more important than our relationship."

She opens her mouth to add something, something important, I can tell by her expression. But the Marquis beats her to it.

The door swings open and slams against the wall.

"Ten minutes are up. You can leave."

Charlotte glares at him. "Are you really so afraid that my sister might find out what a sick game you're playing? Why don't you just admit that you tried to kiss me?" She walks slowly towards him. I'm afraid for her. "We all know you're a deceitful jerk. The only question is why? Why did you make a move on me when you not only have a wife, but even a mistress? Why me too? Because you can never get enough?"

He remains unfazed. "You seem to completely misjudge my taste. I'm into honest women, so you're definitely not my type."

She puts a hand on his shoulder.

I'm left breathless. No one dares to do that. She's the bravest person I know and she doesn't even fear death. "Who do you think she would choose if she had to decide between a toxic fake husband and her own sister, with whom she grew up?"

His face remains unchanged, cool and distant. "We'll have no choice but to wait for the moment when she's faced with the choice." He looks at me. "I am sure she will make the right decision." He steps aside and gestures towards the open door. "If I may."

Charlotte turns to me one last time. "I love you. Don't let him deceive and manipulate you." And she's gone.

The Marquis stands in the doorway. "I know it's hard," he says without looking at me, "but you can't trust anyone. Even if you'd give your life for her, do not expect that she would do the same for you. Trust no one. Not her, not me… only yourself."

And he too dissolves into mist.

A NOBLE CONTRACT

THURSDAY
The Marquis

Her mother took her own life. I didn't have the heart to tell her.

There are more important things to worry about now than the de Guise family's ordeal. Gino has tried to call me twice but I was stuck in a meeting and I know he hates being ignored.

I dial his number. He doesn't pick up. It's his way of showing that he doesn't obey me. He wants to set the pace, but he can forget about that.

I ignore his calls throughout the day, only in the evening, after silently eating with Louise and then taking a shower, do I reach for my phone again.

This time he answers immediately. Dirty bastard. "Jerome, my son. How are you? I was afraid something had happened to you after not hearing from you for so long."

"Given our age difference, you won't live to see the day when I pass away. Unless you're lucky. As they say, luck is with the foolish."

He lets out a dry laugh. "You have courage. I'll give you that."

"Says the one who constantly dares to threaten me - or is that no longer courage, but already foolishness?"

"Who's talking about threats? We have an

agreement, and I want to make sure everything goes flawlessly. Business, nothing more."

"I've already assured you that you'll get Louise on Sunday. What more do you want?"

"Details."

Of course. He's nervous. It unsettles him that I'm offering him what's mine on a silver platter. The whole thing seems too good to be true. I can't blame him; men like us are rightfully suspicious.

"Where will the handover take place?" he asks, taking a sip, probably of alcohol, to calm his nerves.

"Handover? Do you want to keep her, Gino? I thought you wanted to kill her?"

"Maybe I'll reconsider and make her my wife. Louise is a pretty thing; I want to keep all my options open."

It takes all my willpower not to locate him on the spot, grab him, and throw him to my hunting dogs as prey. "Watch your words. She's still my wife."

"She will surely be grateful to you when she finds out how well you fulfilled your marital duties and protected her."

I grit my teeth. "However. The... *handover* will take place at my castle. In the Hall of Mirrors."

"You don't really think I'd willingly enter your estate, do you? I may be old, but not senile yet. At your home, you could shoot me without witnesses. I'm not falling for that."

My anger grows. "Then forget it and grab her if you happen to encounter her on the street. Oh no, I forgot, I've placed her under house arrest." My throat is dry. "Her sister has become suspicious. She's trying to convince her that I'm up to something, and Louise values her word a lot. If I suddenly allow her to leave the estate, she'll become suspicious."

He lets out a heavy sigh, one that speaks of all the years of tricks and games that have eaten dark holes into his soul.

I wonder if I will end up like him, bitter and vengeful, and push away the thought that I might already be.

"You're right, my son. We shouldn't make it any more complicated. I'll be at your door on Sunday at 6 pm. I won't ring the bell. You open the door, and we won't speak a word so she doesn't hear my voice and get the idea to flee or hide. Keep her occupied with something beforehand to ensure she's in the Hall of Mirrors. Lock all doors except the one we enter through. And then decide if you want to watch as I end her life." He laughs. "You can do it for me too, boy, if you feel like it. You would earn my eternal respect."

"Agreed," I say curtly - and hang up.

There's no turning back now.

This is the end.

SATURDAY

The Marquis is going to travel. According to him, he will be out of the country for a few weeks, but he refuses to go into detail about his trip. Every time I ask him about it, he puts me off and attributes his reticence to business matters that would bore me to death.

But I know something is not right.

He is even cooler than usual, more distant - and even though I want to blame it on the fact that Charlotte unexpectedly showed up at our place, even though I want to believe that it means nothing when he avoids my gaze, I still feel that something dark is lurking behind all this.

A storm is brewing.

On Monday, he will leave. His suitcases are not yet packed, but he usually does that at the last minute.

Madison has disappeared from the castle. The Marquis apparently told the truth when he said he had separated from her. Her rooms are empty when I secretly open the door in the afternoon. She is gone.

I didn't dare to bring up the kiss he tried to force on my sister - because I'm afraid of the truth, afraid that he might be honest and confess to me that she appeals to him and that I was nothing more than a wrong decision he regrets.

A knock interrupts my thoughts, gentle and timid

- definitely not the Marquis.

"Come in," I call, and Lola enters. During the months I have spent here, she has grown close to my heart.

We don't speak much since the Marquis is usually in the room when I encounter her, when she serves us food or opens doors for us, but I like her. I have good intuition, and her smile has been warm from the very first moment. Inviting.

"Madame, the Marquis asked me to bring this to you," she says shyly.

I've already asked her countless times to simply call me Louise, but it doesn't come out of her mouth.

Her mother served the Colbert family, and before that her grandmother. Serving is written into her DNA, and I wonder if there's even a possibility that we will become friends one day or if the gulf between rich and poor will forever separate us.

She holds a golden tray in her hands. I reach for the card on it. The Marquis's handwriting, calligraphy inked onto the paper.

"I would like to take you out for dinner tonight - as a farewell before I leave. The driver will be waiting for us at eight o'clock. J."

It must be a long trip he's preparing for if he's planning an official farewell.

Or maybe... I mean more to him than he's willing to admit, and the thought of not having me around for weeks is difficult for him.

I nod at Lola and try to muster a smile, even though it probably looks more like a sad clown.

"Thank you. Please convey my thanks to him and tell him that I will be on time."

As I get ready, shave my legs, and apply perfume, I feel so lonely, so cut off from the world that I finally call Gabriel. Something I should have done a long time ago.

"Louise!" he exclaims after the first ring, and the warm sound of his voice takes some of the burden off my heart. "Are you okay? I haven't heard from you since…"

Since my husband knocked you unconscious. We both dare not say it.

"You don't know how sorry I am."

Gabriel is the most relaxed person I know, but confronted with the Marquis, even he reaches his limits. "Why didn't you call to ask how I was doing?"

"I didn't dare. I was too afraid you might be mad at me."

"Call me crazy, but I understand you."

I catch my breath. "Really?"

"Yes. You're always thinking about others. About the chaos your father caused, the excessive demands of your mother that you could never meet. About your sister's survival, the guilt that burdens your husband. Have you ever stopped and wondered if they worry about you as much as you worry about them?"

"My father tried to make amends for his mistakes…"

"But if his family had been more important to him than money, he wouldn't have taken the risk of turning Gino against you."

"Maybe. But Mother did everything to save our lives."

"Did she? If I see it correctly, she mainly wanted one thing - to marry you off to a respectable man to cleanse the family's reputation. Be completely honest with yourself, Louise. Was it about you, you as a person, or about your reputation?"

"I don't know…"

"You know it. I can't say anything about Charlotte, I like her. But you took on too much by trying to undo what your father did. Saving their lives was a task you weren't up to. None of us would have been strong or powerful enough for that."

I have to swallow. "You speak as if it's already decided that she will die."

It takes a while before he continues. "Maybe everything will turn out for the best. But it will be easier for you to deal with everything if you assume the worst."

It hurts to hear that, but a part of me knows that Gabriel is right, that he's the voice of reason and only wants to help me.

"Think about what *you* want. What *you* need. You haven't done that for too long. If you could choose freely from all possibilities, what would your future look like?"

I have the choice between a lilac chiffon dress, which is high-necked and exudes innocence, and a designer piece made of black satin, floor-length but leaving most of my back and a dangerous amount of bare chest exposed.

On normal evenings, I would choose the first option, but after my conversation with Gabriel and considering the fact that the Marquis will be gone for weeks, I take the bold path.

I want to burn my image into his thoughts, into his memory, and I want him to think of me every night before going to sleep when an ocean separates us.

A glance in the mirror and I'm convinced that this plan will work. I look stunning.

My long hair falls in chocolate waves over my shoulders. A delicate pearl necklace adorns my neck, giving the simple outfit an elegant touch. The dress embraces me in all the right places.

The driver opens the door to the limousine promptly at eight, and I climb into the back seat.

My husband has been out of the house all day and has let me know through Rousel that he'll be waiting for me at the restaurant.

About forty minutes pass before the skyline of Paris appears before us, glowing and shimmering, timeless and sublim. The view reminds me of my school days when I drove into the city daily, fell asleep in class early in the morning, and ate with my friends in front of the Louvre during lunch break.

After my graduation, my visits to the capital became increasingly rare because I was tired of squeezing past crowds of tourists and paying seven euros for a croissant. But as I now catch sight of Paris from a distance, a long-forgotten bloom blossoms in my heart.

At first, I believe the Marquis has reserved a table for us at the Eiffel Tower, but my gut feeling tells me that it's not intimate enough for him.

Due to his position and the fact that wherever he goes all eyes are on him - whether because people know him or simply because they are intimidated by his aura - he loves to find hidden places that belong only to him.

The car stops not far from the Eiffel Tower in front of a six-story building with a perfectly preserved historic facade.

The cool night air bites into my bare skin. Fortunately, I have brought a cardigan, the white cashmere one that the Marquis bought for me and which is as soft as no other piece of clothing I own. By now, my entire wardrobe consists of gifts from the Marquis, and as much as I initially resisted wearing what he paid for, I must admit that he has excellent taste.

In front of me is a restaurant that looks unassuming at first glance and beautiful at second. Not a single guest sits inside, but all the tables are set, I can see from outside, and the lights are on - small lanterns snaking along the ceiling.

It reminds me of one of the restaurants that you usually find outside of Paris, in rural areas towards the sea, owned by the same family for generations. The food found there is authentic and simple, without much show, without unnecessary appetizers that taste bland and are completely overpriced.

It reminds me of childhood, of trips to the sea with my grandparents.

The driver sets the car in motion and disappears. Shyly, I open the door to the restaurant.

The waiter comes towards me, smiles, and bows. "Madame de Colbert, it is an honor to welcome you here." He takes my jacket off.

"Thank you very much." My voice sounds hoarse. "Is the Marquis already here?"

"He is waiting for you on the terrace. I will escort you."

"Thank you, I can find my way alone."

It's only when the waiter locks the entrance door behind me that I realize why the restaurant is empty. The Marquis has booked it for tonight. He wanted to be completely alone with me.

Following the helpful gesture of the waiter, I go up the creaking wooden stairs to the first floor. It smells of garlic, fresh mussels, and fireplace. Here too, all tables are set but empty. Not a soul in sight.

The doors to the terrace are open.

There he is.

With his back to me.

Leaning forward on the railing and yet so tall that from my viewpoint, it could seem like he's touching the stars.

His hair blows in the wind.

He reminds me of old paintings, showing solitary wanderers, in harmony with nature, but always on the run from themselves.

"Come closer," he says before turning to face me. He heard my steps. "You look beautiful as always."

We see each other every day, yet he manages to miraculously charge every encounter with electricity, as if it were the first.

My knees tremble, and I struggle not to stumble in my high heels.

The Marquis reaches out his arm. I take his hand.

The scene is so magical that no words can do it justice. Hundreds of candles are scattered across the terrace, on the railing, on the tables, on the ground. The warm golden flames dance in the wind. Lanterns glow above our heads. The night air is cold, but large heat lamps are installed above us, so that I begin to sweat in my cashmere jacket after just a few seconds.

The Marquis looks deep into my eyes. "I'm glad you came."

"Why wouldn't I?"

"I was worried that your sister might have influenced you."

He must read from my face how my mood shifts, as he quickly steers the conversation to another topic. "I really enjoyed the night in the pavilion with you. It felt right to share this secret place with you - and that's why I want to give you a proper farewell before I leave. One that does justice to all the months we've spent together."

What he says sounds final. As if it's a farewell forever.

Quickly, I shake off the thought and start unbuttoning my jacket. The Marquis follows the movements of my fingers with his eyes.

"Are you undressing already? I knew you were bold, but wanting to skip so many steps at once…?"

Laughing, I playfully punch him on the shoulder. This time, I'm smart enough not to do it with full force. I won't hurt my hand on his steel muscles again.

He takes my jacket and hands it to the waiter, who has magically appeared beside us. Then he pulls out a chair and lets me sit at the table with a view, that I never want to forget.

The Eiffel Tower sparkles so close to us that I want to reach out my hand to test if I can touch it. Tourists look down at us from the elevator that carries them to the top. I can't blame them for their curiosity - the Marquis has chosen a place for tonight like something out of a fairy tale.

He takes a seat across from me. The waiter pours us water. Nervously, I take a sip. "How long will you be traveling?"

"Weeks, maybe months - it depends on how the negotiations go." He touches my hand, which is resting on the table. "But let's not talk about work tonight."

"I still have one question left that you promised to answer."

He smiles. "Do you want to ask it tonight?"

"It depends on how the evening goes."

The wind carries a hint of his scent to me. He smells masculine and rich.

"I would also like to ask you a question, Louise, if that's okay with you." His hand still touches mine, and the warmth of his thumb burns into my skin. A picture flickers in my mind, of the Marquis' crest on my chest, and I quickly push it away. The waiter takes our order, then leaves us alone.

"Go ahead."

He releases his grip, leans back in his chair, crosses his arms. His gaze wanders over the starry sky, as if searching for something, perhaps an answer to life's mysterious questions.

"Have you been able to enjoy past few months at all? Or has it just been terrible for you?"

"Are we talking about the months during which my family was hunted, I was forced to marry a stranger and lost my parents?"

"Forgive me, I didn't mean to be insensitive."

"It's okay." I wave it off with a fleeting gesture. "I know what you actually mean. And no, it wasn't all terrible. Honestly, at first, I found it hard to get used to you. Your bossy manner and your stubbornness." He smiles warmly. "But over time, I realized that you're just playing a role, that you were expected from a young age to burn the world down and that deep down you are good."

"How do you know that?"

Nervously, I pick at a piece of skin that has come loose from my nail bed. It stings, but the pain helps me keep a clear head.

"You were always there. In every moment I needed you. When my father was shot, you saved me from the line of fire and held me in your arms on the way home. You convinced Dane Gilbertson to meet with Charlotte, even though it was a risk - and even though it didn't end particularly well" - he looks like he has to suppress a laugh - "... I still appreciate your efforts."

"You accompanied me to my father's funeral," I continue. "You supported me when I had barely any strength left to walk. Even though you were cold to me and left me alone too often, deep down I knew all along that you were there for me. That a call was enough and you would get on a plane to find me."

He swallows. "What if I told you that I'm not the person you think I am?"

"Then I would know that you're lying to yourself. Your eyes give you away, Jerome. You may be a gifted actor, but deep down in your soul, you hold a soft heart captive."

"Wow," he laughs. "I should get that tattooed."

And we both laugh. It feels like a weight has been lifted off my shoulders as I bask in his laughter.

I breathe in the night air deeply - I want to keep the memory of this evening forever within me.

"A man like me can't afford to fall in love," he says, suddenly serious again. "The men in my family marry to preserve their bloodline, but we don't give away our hearts."

"On principle?"

"Out of caution."

"Out of fear of being hurt?"

"Out of fear of what can happen to the women who become part of our family."

I shudder.

"Power always looks impressive from the outside. You've been told that I - as the head of the Circle - am untouchable, that no one would dare to harm me. And it's true." He plays with his fork, the only sign that he too is nervous. "My enemies can't kill me, but they would find a way to wound me fatally, so deeply that I would withdraw on my own accord. And they would do that by taking away from me the one person who means more to me than all the billions in the account."

His gaze captures me.

I dissolve.

The wind carries my soul away.

"If I were to admit to myself that I love you... then I would be lost. Then I would not sleep a wink at night, fearing someone might slit your throat while you sleep, then during every important conversation, I would only think about where you are, with whom, and whether you could be in danger. Loving you would destroy me."

"But not loving me destroys you too. Only you're alone in it."

He avoids my gaze. His knuckles are white.

"I tried. When you told me you wanted to be my wife, truly be my wife, for a moment I made the decision to give you what you deserve. Honest love."

The word sounds foreign on his tongue. Has he ever told a woman that he loves her?

"But when you wanted to sleep with me, when your naked warm body pressed against mine, I lost my mind for a moment. For the first time, I felt what it means to lose control over myself."

Goosebumps run down my arms.

"I wanted to grab you and fuck you sore. Destroy you and put you back together. I wanted you to belong to me, entirely. And when you looked up at me, I felt fear. Fear for you. That's when I understood that I shouldn't cross that line. That it would destroy us both."

A shadow moves in the corner of my eye. I look inside the restaurant and spot two waiters with plates on their arms, looking unsure if they should interrupt our conversation.

With a forced smile, I reassure them that they need not be shy. The scent of mussels and pasta wafts into my nose. It smells delicious, but my mouth tastes like ash and death.

"I would be willing to take that risk." Neither of us

touches the food. "But I would never be willing to lose you. I would have to burn the world down and set paradise ablaze if anything happened to you. And something will happen to you by my side. Today or in ten years. It *will* happen."

He clenches the tablecloth.

"That's why, Louise, I will not open my heart to you. Our beginning would be your end."

I swallow, wanting to say something, but he continues. "Whatever I do, I exaggerate. I am too harsh with my opponents, too merciless with my enemies. I have brought too much pain into the world, more than was ever necessary. That's why I know that I would also exaggerate with my love. I would protect you too much, possess you too much, and fuck you too often. You'd get crushed under all the burden that I carry in my heart."

Before he can continue, I quickly raise a hand and motion for him to be silent. "Don't you think you wallow a bit too much in self-pity?"

I would give anything to capture his surprised expression in a photo.

"You keep telling yourself the same story over and over: that you're damned to live alone in the dark. That you can't be happy and your touch hurts. Have you ever considered that all your excuses are just masking one simple truth: that you're afraid your feelings won't be reciprocated?"

He blinks.

"The Marquis is speechless. I feel honored."

He runs a hand through his hair. The shadows of the night and the lights of the Eiffel Tower dance across his face. I catch my breath at his beauty.

"Would you reciprocate them?" he finally asks. He looks into the distance, as if it's easier for him to speak the words when he doesn't look at me.

"I know that loving you is not easy. But I would try every day anew."

"Why?"

"Because we're connected. When I'm near you, I feel complete. I firmly believe that it was no coincidence that we met each other."

The softness disappears, his expression becomes hard, merciless. "You're deluding yourself."

Reflexively, I pull my hand back. "What is that supposed to mean?"

"That you believe in fairy tales."

My fork scrapes across the still untouched plate. It's a shame to waste food and the pasta smells mouth-watering, so I start eating. It tastes like nothing, even though I know it's delicious.

"Then what's the point of this evening?" I gesture to the ambiance surrounding us. "Why are you dining with me as if we were a couple, saying beautiful things and trying to please me? If you don't intend to have a real relationship with me?"

He drinks his wine in one gulp. "As I said before. I wanted to say goodbye."

A sudden feeling of fear creeps into my bones, an uneasiness whose origin I cannot explain. My fingers start to tremble. "Will you come back?" I hope to catch a glimpse of his true feelings, but the icy mask sits perfectly.

"Of course. The castle is my home."

"I don't believe you." Something in his tone makes me suspicious. His posture is too rigid, his jaw too tense. "Is this some kind of breakup? Do you want a divorce?" Determined, I push my chair back.

"Don't talk nonsense. Of course not."

"Then tell me what's wrong. Something is not right, I know it."

He closes his green eyes, flares his nostrils, trying not to lose control. "You're overreacting. Everything is fine."

A tear forms in the corner of my eye, but I don't allow it to escape. He's not worth a single tear.

"Nothing is good at all," I hiss. "Because you're a coward and a liar. You can't even tell the truth once, always hiding things and playing a role."

My fingernails dig into my thigh. I jump up from the chair. "Maybe I was wrong. Maybe you *are* exactly the cold, heartless person you show to the world."

Then everything suddenly happens very quickly. He jumps up, pushes his chair back so hard that it falls to the ground with a loud crash and stands close to me.

His hands grab my wrists, his hot body presses against mine. He takes a step forward, then another, baring his teeth, until the cold metal of the railing presses into my skin. Below us lay the streets of Paris,

I hear cars honking and can only wonder if he will push me into the depths. If he will claim it was an accident.

"Do you not believe that I tried?" His eyes speak of fear and pain. "I tried so damn hard that it almost destroyed me. I *want* to be good for you, I *want* to show you how much I care, but I am cursed."

The wind carries away all the words that were on the tip of my tongue moments ago. My breath is heavy. His face is so close to mine that I'm convinced he will kiss me. Instead, he pulls me close and hugs me so tightly, so tenderly, that for a moment I believe in a happy ending. His fingertips brush over my bare back. I shudder. He growls.

"In another life, I would have given you the love you deserve. I'm sorry, Louise. I'm so sorry."

His fingertips dig through my wind-tousled hair. He strokes my head. A gentle kiss on my forehead. A sigh so heavy, it sounds like centuries of accumulated pain, broken dreams, and the hopeless search for peace of mind.

The Marquis is a restless man. It was foolish of me to believe I could be the place where he finds peace.

My throat is dry. When I speak, it sounds strange. "Promise me you will come back?"

He takes my face in both cold, large hands, tilts my head back, and forces me to look into his eyes. "I promise. I will come back." I can't discern any dishonesty in his expression.

"Why do you desperately want to convince me to

love you?" he asks softly. The night carries away his voice before it can wrap around my heart. Our gazes still embrace each other.

It feels so wrong to want to save him - from his enemies, from himself - because I know he is the villain in this story, that he's the one spinning intrigues and killing people while I sleep and dream of him. Maybe there's something wrong with me.

Or maybe I've had enough of broken things always being left behind, of only heroes getting their own stories and imperfection always being deemed bad.

Maybe I'm deluding myself.

But maybe he awakens the beautiful things in me, courage and hope, without even knowing it.

"I don't need to convince you," I reply. "I already know that you love me."

"And why should that be?"

"Because I'm the only person who has ever believed in you."

"Many people have believed in me. My father always believed that I would be strong enough to lead the Circle. Your father believed that I could save his family. My friends believe in me by foolishly trusting me. Why should you be special?"

"Because only I believe that you're good. I don't believe in your money or power. I believe in your heart." My index finger wanders to his chest and I tap the tip against the smooth fabric of his suit. "The heart that you have long since given up on."

He releases my face, turns away. His broad shoulders tremble - or am I just imagining it? He leans on the railing. His gaze drifts over the nighttime backdrop of the city. "May I ask you for a promise?"

"That depends on the promise," I say.

He turns to face me. His long fingers thoughtfully trace the contours of his lips. "Promise me to keep that feeling inside you. The thought that I can be good and that I haven't always been bad to you."

Slowly, he approaches me and places his index finger under my chin. "If I disappoint you, don't just think poorly of me. Remember that we had beautiful moments and days where a happy ending didn't seem so impossible. Can you promise me that?"

I nod silently. And he kisses me. Not demanding, not hungry.

Gentle.

His lips form a secret that is meant only for me.

It reaches my heart.

Because I don't know that tomorrow I must die.

SUNDAY

Despite the Marquis' words, I've never believed in fairy tales.

I've never dared to hope to determine my own life. Instead, I accepted early on that my paths are predetermined, that I cannot dream like other girls, and that while my title gives me all the money in the world, it does not give me the opportunity to use it for meaningful things.

I never waited for a prince to rescue me. When my parents presented me with the facts and explained that I would marry the Marquis, I accepted my fate without believing that things would turn out for the better.

Fairy tales are for dreamers.

I no longer want to lose myself in hopes.

I want to take action.

My flight leaves in three and a half hours. My suitcase is packed. Gabriel will arrive in a few minutes with his car to pick me up so we drive to the airport together.

Last night, I spontaneously booked a trip to Portugal. For as long as I can remember, I've wanted to learn how to surf, and the thought of riding wild waves and becoming one with the ocean makes breathing easier for me, while the thick walls of the castle seem to be closing in on me.

I can't stay here. I love him. And unrequited love is

the deadliest poison of all.

The sound of the zipper feels like freedom as I close my suitcase. I've packed very little, only things that won't give the Marquis any clue about where I'm going.

He can't find me. This morning, I secretly withdrew some cash and I plan to find a job in Portugal, maybe in a bar or a cute café.

My parents never allowed me to work. Now is the time to stand on my own two feet. Far away from dominant men, designer clothes, and blood money in the bank.

My phone lights up. A message from Gabriel. *Hey, I'm leaving now and will be there in about 40 minutes. See you soon.*

I won't lie - leaving the Marquis hurts. Not because I will have a target on my back and live in constant fear of running into Gino's people on the street. It hurts to leave his scent behind, the brief moments when his eyes soften, and the quiet encounters where we don't speak much yet I still feel understood.

But he clearly told me to my face. He cannot give me what I need. What I deserve.

My suitcase is heavy, but I don't pull it behind me, afraid of making too much noise and drawing the Marquis' attention to me. He leaves tomorrow. So I grab the handle of the heavy bag and drag it through corridors, up stairs, and down to the ground floor.

Today everything is eerily quiet. Normally, I

encounter countless servants carrying food through the corridors, pushing dining cars, or flying past with urgent messages to deliver.

Today the castle is deserted. No voices, no footsteps. The horses were not let out in the morning. On the ground floor, near the kitchen, there is no smell of food, even though it's already past noon.

Something is not right. This silence is unnatural. As if a dark beast were lurking around the next corner, ready to pounce.

Nonsense. I'm getting paranoid because I've spent too many months alone with myself. Probably the servants are just in another part of the castle, the west wing or outside in the courtyard.

Not wanting to tempt fate, I descend the narrow, damp steps to one of the back entrances and have to concentrate hard not to slip on the wet stone. The strap of the suitcase cuts into my skin. Ten steps, four steps, one step. Made it.

Relieved, I sigh, reach for the doorknob and... locked. Damn. I furrow my brow in surprise. Rousel always opens the door in the morning to receive deliveries. But he was probably busy with something else today or he's sick? Still strange.

A desperate sigh escapes me as I realize that I have to drag the heavy suitcase back up all those stairs. I start moving.

A few sweaty minutes later, I am back where I started.

Taking the main entrance would be too risky. The

Marquis uses it frequently and often conducts business calls on the grand staircase. I don't want to run into him. He would only try to convince me not to leave, and unfortunately, I'm too susceptible to his charm.

So through the gardens it is. I have to hurry. Gabriel and I have arranged for him to wait for me about a mile from the castle, so that no one sees his car and becomes suspicious.

It rained last night, and the ground is soft and muddy, which will make it difficult for me to move forward with the suitcase. I don't have much time left.

I haven't used the tall glass doors that lead directly into the gardens often, but by now I know my way around the vast building well and stand before the exits just a few seconds later.

The first door is locked.

So is the second.

My pulse begins to quicken.

This is strange.

Struggling to keep a cool head, I try the next door. Locked. No. This can't be. He can't know that I'm leaving.

And yet, something is not right. I am trapped here. The staff is gone.

Suddenly, I feel sick. A peculiar sense fills the air, a charged and expectant silence that I only know from hunting, when my father took me into the woods and we crouched wordlessly behind bushes, our eyes fixed on a deer that was unaware of its impending death.

Goosebumps run down my back. Suddenly, I feel like I'm being watched.

There's only one way to find out if I'm really trapped here. The main entrance. It's always open. If that door is locked too, then I will know for sure that something is wrong. That I'm stuck in a trap.

The Marquis is dangerous, a mocking voice sings in my head. *You always knew, but didn't want to acknowledge it.*

The farewell he spoke of yesterday... I feel sick. I walk quickly through the corridor.

He wouldn't lie to me.

But would he?

He wouldn't hurt me.

Are you sure about that?

The doors to the mirror hall are closed. With a pounding heart, I push against them. They open. Thank goodness.

Just a few more steps.

The wheels of the suitcase echo through the hall. I'm surrounded by mirrors, reflecting me hundreds of times. Hundreds of anxious faces watching me as I flee.

The door leading out of the hall is close.

Breathe, Louise, breathe. Everything is okay.

Relief warms me from within as I take the final step - and pure shock freezes me as the Marquis appears before me. He looks the same as always, but today he scares me. Maybe it's the locked doors, or perhaps it's the sadness in his eyes as he surveys me from head to toe. I know him angry, determined, cold. But not sad.

"You want to leave me?" he asks, stepping into the hall and closing the door behind him.

He blocks my path.

I don't know what to answer him.

"Without saying goodbye to me first?" He approaches me. I start to walk backwards. He smiles. "I don't want to lock you up, Louise. In the past, I have done that and it was a mistake. I can't clip the wings of a beautiful bird like you."

One step forward.

One step back.

Two hearts beating too fast.

"I don't believe you."

"I promise. You can go. You are free."

"Then get out of my way."

He runs a hand through his hair, and I wonder if he knows that this gesture gets under my skin every time. If he wants to distract and charm me so that I change my mind and stay.

"You put me under house arrest - and now suddenly I am free to go?"

"I may be an arrogant asshole, but I'm also capable of learning from my mistakes."

My hand clings to the suitcase handle. I have to make an effort not to collapse from nervousness.

"You can go, Louise." My name on his lips brings

tears to my eyes, and I wonder if a small lonely part of me has wished he would stop me.

"Thank you," I say curtly and start moving again.

When I reach for the doorknob, it doesn't move.

The Marquis has locked it...

"Let's toast to the past months as a farewell."

I turn to him. He stands next to a serving trolley, which I hadn't noticed before.

Two champagne glasses and a bottle are arranged on it, which he has just uncorked. A loud pop and white foam begins to spill out.

"I'm not in the mood," I say.

"Just a sip," he insists.

With a sigh, I let go of my suitcase and approach the Marquis. He won't give up if he doesn't get his way.

Gabriel will arrive soon, and if we want to catch our flight, I have no choice but to comply.

The Marquis is in the process of filling the two glasses. A lump forms in my throat. All of this feels like a fever dream.

He looks at me, his gaze so full of tenderness that I briefly consider canceling my trip and staying, hoping that one day he will overcome his fears and open up to me.

But I am worth more. "I deserve to be chosen," it shoots out of me uncontrollably.

He smiles gently. "You do. You deserve all the good in this world. That's why I'm not the right one for you."

He hands me a glass. We toast. The sound resonates within me, wraps around my heart, and reminds me that no man in this world will ever be as impressive and strong as the one standing before me at this moment, and yet I have no choice but to leave if I want to be happy.

"You have made my life so much more beautiful," he says. "Your hopeful eyes looked at me, and for a moment, I believed that even a man like me could deserve a happy ending. I am rich and powerful, but a king is nothing without his queen."

He leans forward. His scent fills my nose. I want this moment to never end.

As he gently presses his lips against mine, he condemns me to an eternity of longing. I will always think of him and compare every man to him.

His tongue caresses me.

His soul nestles against mine.

And two seconds later, the moment is already over.

My face burns like fire.

He toasts to me, "To you, Louise."

I raise the glass to my lips. "To us." And I empty it in one gulp.

I need to get out of here. A bitter aftertaste burns on my tongue.

"Open the doors for me."

He smiles again. That's suspicious too. In all these months, I have seen him smile so rarely that I can count it on one hand, and now that I'm leaving, he's giving me one smile after another? It doesn't add up.

"Your wish is my command," he says, but instead of moving towards the doors, he brings his thumb and forefinger of his right hand together, places them between his lips, and whistles so loudly that it almost bursts my eardrums.

Shit.

What's happening here?

A key turns from the outside in the lock.

With wide eyes, I look at the Marquis. "What…?"

A tear. A single lonely tear runs down his cheek. And everything makes sense.

"Traitor."

A NOBLE CONTRACT

*T*he Marquis

"Daddy, Daddy!" I scream so loud that my throat burns.

My father is a small blurry silhouette on the horizon. If he can hear me, he doesn't show it.

The little bird twitches in my hand. Its breath is too fast.

Daddy.

He has to help me.

He has to do something.

The bird can't die.

Just a few minutes ago, it was high in the sky, flying from one tree to another and singing its happy song, and now it's fighting for its life in my trembling hand.

It can't die.

As fast as I can, I run up the hill towards the paddock where my father is standing.

"Daddy, Daddy, Daddy!"

He doesn't even turn his head. My legs burn like fire, my lungs wheeze. I'm suffocating. But I can't stop, I can't, I can't.

There's a reason why I was standing under the tree at that exact moment when the little bird was attacked by a hawk. It's my duty to save its life.

I believe in it.

My little feet carry me over flowers and grasses. It's a warm summer evening. I miss my mother. I run and run and struggle for air - and finally, finally, my father stands before me and I cling to his legs and scream and cry: "You have to help him."

My father is notorious for his merciless gaze. It's said that he can bring his enemies to their knees with a single look.

One would think that this gaze is reserved only for those he hates, but as he looks down at me and cold anger plays on his lips, I wonder if I am not his greatest enemy.

Because he knows that one day I will succeed him.

Because he is afraid that I might become stronger than him.

The bird is still breathing.

It is warm in my hand and its little heart beats fast.

Tears stream down my cheeks.

"Where did you find it?" my father asks with a bored voice, looking disgusted at the helpless animal.

"Under the oak trees. He's still alive. We can save him."

I don't see his hand before it hits me with full force, smashes against my face and almost knocks me to the ground. At the last moment, I regain my balance.

"Boys don't cry." His mouth is just a thin line. He is tall and I shiver in his shadow, even though the sun is still shining.

"Give it to me." He reaches out his hand. I trust him. Even though he hits me. Even though he's never there for me when I need him.

He's my father.

My hero.

I place the bird in his palm. His colorful feathers

shimmer preciously. He's beautiful and he deserves to live.

"Take a good look at it," my father says. "And never forget that anything that makes us soft has the power to destroys us."

And he snaps the bird's neck.

I never cry again.
Not until today.
Over twenty years later.
The first tear since I was a child.
My heart tightens.
I'm so sorry.
My heart.
My everything.
Louise.

A NOBLE CONTRACT

Louise

The key turns twice in the lock, then there's a click, and the door opens.

Gino enters, followed by Madison. They are both impeccably dressed. Gino is wearing a tailored black suit, and Madison is in a tight dress that accentuates her perfect silhouette. The Marquis is also dressed in black. They have coordinated this. This is my funeral.

Madison wears such a self-satisfied smile on her face that it turns my stomach. I refuse to look at the Marquis; instead, my full attention is on the two people who will be my end if I don't manage to escape.

"Young love," says Gino. "It can make life so much more beautiful, but it can also blind us to what's happening right under our noses."

Madison closes the door. Someone locks it from the outside. They outnumber me.

Gino walks calmly towards me. I've never seen him in person before. Father has spoken of him, Mother has forbidden his name in our house, and I didn't want to believe that he really exists, but there he stands, flesh and blood, breathing and grinning, ready to complete his work.

"It's almost tragic. How naively you lost your heart to him," he gestures towards the Marquis, but my gaze doesn't follow his hand.

I want to forever forget that he exists and never

look into his eyes again.

"I could almost pity you if you hadn't tried to continue your father's games and deceive me."

I gasp in shock. He's getting closer. It's hard to tell how old he is. His face is tanned by the sun. Deep wrinkles run through his skin. All his sins are etched in his expression, in the corners of his mouth, which slyly curve upwards, and in the flaring of his nostrils, giving him a constant disdainful look.

He's better dressed than I would have thought. In my mind, he wore a leather jacket and ripped jeans, but in reality, he is no less of a gentleman than the Marquis. Or pretends to be.

On his left hand, he wears a ring. Not a wedding ring, but the seal of the Circle. The Marquis has the same one. I should have known. It was a trick from the beginning. A false game.

The Circle is an ancient covenant. Those who are honored to join it are obligated with their lives to uphold the rules - and the supreme rule states that one does not betray a brother.

Albert has tried to betray Gino. By doing so, he has broken the code of honor.

Of course. That's why the Marquis offered to marry me. It was the easiest way to lure me into a trap. He would never have helped my parents escape Gino's revenge. Rules mean everything to him; they are the foundation of his world. He is helping Gino achieve his revenge.

Without wanting to, my eyes wander to him. His

sight hurts more than any physical wound I have ever received. His face looks tormented. Tightly pressed lips and deep furrows on his forehead. An all-consuming shadow lies on him, a darkness that I have not known in him before: despair.

He looks as if he has to force himself to remain calm. His muscles are tense, his eyes so wild that I begin to fear him. Truly fear - not hopefully, not interested, but panicked and breathless. I feel sick.

My stomach makes a gurgling sound.

Gino is now standing too close to me. "Did you really think I wouldn't find out what you were planning? Marrying off your sister to protect her from me?"

My eyes wander from him to the Marquis. "You miserable traitor? You told him?"

The Marquis says nothing. Someone else answers in his place, and when I recognize the voice, my little world collapses forever. "No, *I* told him."

Charlotte enters the room through a hidden door in the wall. She looks the same as always, with her pale skin and strong features, my sister, my confidante who has accompanied every step and hope of my past.

But she is not the Charlotte I know. Her nose is too proudly raised towards the sky, her chin pushed too arrogantly forward. I nearly collapse to my knees.

"Charlotte?" My mouth hangs open.

"Isn't this a wonderful surprise?" Gino beams and spreads his arms. "A family reunion."

Charlotte stands next to Madison. *No no no no no.* She's wearing a black dress. A cursed, all-destroying, black dress.

"What are you doing?" I ask her.

She shrugs. "I had no other choice." She seems almost bored. Completely indifferent, she meets my desperate gaze.

I turn my attention back to Gino. I can't bear the sight of Charlotte by Madison's side. "What do you have against her?"

"You think I'm blackmailing her?"

"I can't think of any other reason why she should be here. With you."

It has to be the reason. I want to add something more, but my tongue is dry and heavy. I have to save my words.

"You really *are* in the dark. Delightful." Gino's feigned friendliness is unbearable. He doesn't reveal how exactly he plans to kill me.

"Your sister has one thing to gain if she stands by my side. Her life."

The mirrored hall begins to spin. Gino's contours blur slightly.

"She found me - and she was lucky. The day she stood at my door, I happened to be in a good mood. So I listened to her offer."

I shake my head. "You're lying."

"Ask her yourself." He reaches out an arm and gestures in her direction. Charlotte looks almost sad as our eyes meet, our same bright eyes, through which strangers have always recognized that we are sisters.

"Please tell me that's not true," I beg her.

"I'm sorry." Her previously composed facade crumbles. A hint of compassion flickers behind her cold expression, but it disappears too quickly for me to grasp and wake her up.

"What have you done?" My voice sounds strange. Speaking is difficult. My fingers tingle.

"I had to do it. You couldn't find a way to save me. I didn't know how else to survive."

I shake my head in disbelief. "And so you went to Gino and allied with him?"

"I gave him all the business secrets that Albert kept in his office. All the files, all the documents. They are worth millions."

"More than my life?"

She trembles. "What about *my* life, Louise? How much is my life worth? Our parents married you instead of saving me. No one fought for me. So I had to take matters into my own hands."

She takes a deep breath and closes her eyes. "I will never forgive myself for what I have done, you better believe me. But if I hadn't betrayed what you were planning to Gino, he would have killed me."

"And you think now he will let you live?"

"I gave him everything I had left. You, our father's secrets, even mother's jewelry. If that's not enough…"

"It will never be enough for him. A man driven by revenge always demands more."

Charlotte stares at the ground.

"And her?" I point to Madison. "What does she have to do with all this?"

Gino is now standing so close to me that he can touch me. He puts an arm around my shoulders. "Madison is my niece. Didn't you know that?"

My right foot is numb. I shift my weight to the left. Gino looks feignedly surprised at the Marquis.

"You didn't tell her? That your girlfriend is part of my family?"

"She's no longer my girlfriend," he growls back.

Madison doesn't flinch, but I know it's driving her crazy inside. At least one thing the Marquis didn't lie about.

"She watched you while she still lived here. Before he," his finger points disdainfully at the Marquis, "had nothing better to do than throw her out the door. Until then everything was going well. Madison reported every step of yours to me. I always knew where you were and where I could meet you if I wanted to kill you."

"But when Madison moved out, I needed a new informant," he continues. "And your lovely sister came in handy."

Something is wrong with my circulation. I need to sit down. Powerlessly, I sink to my knees.

"I despised Albert," Gino hisses. "And it wouldn't even occur to me in my dreams to let his useless offspring live. I will be the one to wipe out his bloodline."

My upper body sags forward. With both hands, I catch myself and lean on the ground.

Gino's words echo in my dazed head.

Our bloodline.

A cold bolt of realization jolts through me. I sit up and immediately stagger back. I crash ungracefully onto the parquet floor with my elbows.

"Charlotte! He tricked you."

He wants to wipe out our bloodline.

He won't spare her.

All color has drained from Charlotte's face. "You…" She points at him with a trembling finger. "I gave you everything I could."

He just smiles and shakes his head. "That was not enough."

"Take me, but spare her!" I wail.

He looks at me gravely. "I'll take both of you."

And he signals to the Marquis. The man I believed to love steps forward.

"No no no… please no," I sob. He gives me a single regretful look and pulls the trigger. I scream.

My scream pierces through worlds and past centuries. All the pain that people ever felt gathers in my chest and tears me apart. Consuming, merciless pain.

Charlotte's body is just a shell, a memory of what once was.

I close my eyes.

A NOBLE CONTRACT

Louise

She is two and a half years younger than me, but two centimeters taller.

Mother marks lines on the kitchen wall every six months. In recent months, Charlotte has overtaken me.

When you're small, everything revolves around getting bigger.

Daddy says that once we're adults, we will long for childhood.

I don't believe him.

Adults are free.

I want to be free.

Charlotte sticks her tongue out at me. She holds my favorite doll in both hands and because she's stronger than me, she knows I can't snatch it from her.

"Give it back to me. Right now!" I scream with a whiny voice.

"Come and get it," Charlotte grins and then her legs in pink tights start moving. She can run so fast that it almost looks like she's flying.

For ten breaths, I try to catch up with her. On the eleventh, I blink and lose my balance.

My face slams onto the marble floor. Something cracks too loudly. When I open my eyes again, I'm lying in a puddle of blood - it's dripping from my mouth. Instinctively, I touch my teeth with one hand - and I'm shocked.

A tooth with a root lies in front of me on the marble. A

perfect white tooth. It should have accompanied me for a lifetime. Now it lies there, useless and dead.

My shock lasts until Charlotte stands before me with wide eyes. Then the pain sets in.

Tears and blood mix on my cheeks. Panicked, Charlotte strokes my face clean. "I'm sorry, Louise. I'm so sorry. I didn't mean for this to happen Please don't tell mother."

It's not her fault. I knew she runs faster than me. I should have known that I could never catch up with her. Yet, I tried to keep up with her pace, and the blood and pain are the price I now have to pay for it.

I have lost a part of myself.

Charlotte's skull hits the wooden floor with a dull thud. A gash tears her forehead open, but her soul has already left her pretty head, and she feels nothing of the pain.

For that, I feel it all the more.

I always thought that one becomes numb when life exaggerates, that the body has a built-in defense mechanism that makes one indifferent and cold when everything becomes too much.

But every death I have had to endure in the last months has left new painful scars on me.

Charlotte was the only person in the whole world for whom I would have given my life.

I trusted her with every fragment of my soul.

And she betrayed me.

Sold our family secrets to Gino and risked my death to save herself.

And now she is gone.

I have no one left.

My gaze shifts to the Marquis. I pour all the hatred, all the contempt that burns within me, into this one look. I swore never to look at him again, but in this moment, I taste only one promise on my tongue: I will extinguish him.

It's evident that my hatred hurts him. He chews on his lower lip. Good. Pain will be his future. I will turn every miserable second of his remaining life into suffering.

My hands form two determined fists. "I should have known," I hiss.

The Marquis still says nothing.

Instead, Gino laughs even louder. "You should have - and yet you were naive enough to trust a man known for eliminating anything that stands in his way to power. Did you really think you were more important to him than all the others he's taken down before you?"

For two breaths, there is only him and me.

The Marquis.

My husband.

My love.

My end.

And me.

We look at each other. "Yes," I whisper. "Yes, I thought so."

And he grimaces in pain. The weapon in his hand trembles. He briefly closes his eyes. This is my chance.

Swift as the wind that commands the tides, I fly towards him. I have nothing left to lose. My head collides with his stomach, my entire body weight rams against his powerful stature.

Normally, even my gathered strength cannot affect him. I'm a nuisance to him when I try to throw him off balance.

But in this moment, everything is different. Because he's arrogant enough to believe that he has already defeated me, because he closes his eyes and doesn't see me coming.

My blow is unexpected for him. He gasps for air,

staggers backward, immediately regains his composure, but I have two seconds during which I manage to snatch the weapon from his hands.

I learned hunting from my father. He taught me how to handle a weapon properly. Back then, I hated training with him, but right now I'm grateful to him.

My hand hovers unexpectedly calmly in the air. The barrel of the gun aims at the Marquis' face. He remains eerily calm. His breathing is steady. He looks at me, but there is nothing in his eyes, no emotion, no hidden message intended only for me, no *"trust me, this is all not real and I will protect you."*

Gino still laughs. But it sounds less convincing.

I glance at him.

"The girl has some bite, you have to give her that. No wonder you couldn't keep your hands off her, Marquis."

The Marquis clenches his jaw. "Don't speak of her like that."

"And don't you dare defend me," I snap at him. "Not after you sold me out and killed my sister."

Saying it out loud makes it real. Her lifeless body in a pool of blood. I have to look away.

I unexpectedly feel strong. Maybe because her death took the last thing that meant something to me. Now I'm completely alone and know that I must die. Today, even. But I will take as many traitors with me to the grave as possible.

"You don't understand," he says so apathetically that I wish I could rip his heart out of his chest while he's still alive. "I had to do it."

My eye twitches. "The only thing you'll have to do is die."

And I run.

FORTY-SIX

I'm afraid.

Not afraid of dying, but afraid that it was all in vain.

My lungs wheeze as I run like I've never run before. It's true that the survival instinct gives our bodies superhuman strength.

Gino curses. Madison laughs. Not a sound from the Marquis. His heart is made of stone. I'm the mouse foolish enough to walk into his claws. If this day is my end, then I deserve it.

There's only one thought driving me now: the thought of revenge. The idea of paying back all the men who thought they could turn my life into a puppet dance, who dared to interfere with my fate and for whom my death is just one move among many.

I want to see them fall. I want to watch as they lose everything that means something to them, their wealth, their beautiful clothes. I want retribution.

The Marquis has long legs - and they're following me. I can hear the sound of his pursuit.

He's running after me.

A thousand questions race through my mind.

How fast can he run in his tailored suit?

Why did he pretend as if I meant something to him?

How powerful is Gino if he can force the Marquis to kill

me?

Did he even have to force him or is he doing it willingly?

"Louise! Stop. Let's talk about this."

His sweet voice is a deadly trick. He wants to deceive me one last time.

My feet fly even faster over the marble, and I breathe a sigh of relief as I reach a carpeted staircase. On the cold stone, my steps sound too loud, making it easy for him to track me, but on the carpet, it will be harder for him to find me.

Up the stairs. Along the corridor. Around ten corners. Dead end.

My heart races and then skips three beats. I'm trapped.

"Louise. I beg you. It's just a misunderstanding."

I feel sick, not just from running. Even though my endurance leaves much to be desired, my nausea is not due to lack of training. This feels different. My mouth tastes like iron. Like blood.

I cough. Blood splatters on my palm. Everything in me freezes. I spit blood...

The wall in front of me, exhaustion in my bones... I need to find a hiding place where I can hold out long enough to convince the Marquis that I've escaped from the castle. When he sleeps, I will sneak out. But now, my only chance of survival lies in hiding.

Although I've spent months in his castle, I don't even come close to knowing all the rooms. The wing

I'm currently in is unfamiliar to me.

Everything seems older than in my chambers. Centuries-old pieces of furniture are hidden under large white cloths meant to protect them from dust.

Time has stood still here. The air tastes heavy and old. Marble busts watch my every move with empty eyes, waiting for my decision on where to hide.

I don't have many options. A massive wooden wardrobe next to the window could provide enough space to conceal myself, but it's too obvious a hiding spot. That's where the Marquis will look for me first.

Something warm drips from my left nostril. Blood. Drip, drip, drip.

Your time is running out.

This castle is cursed. I don't want to die here. Anywhere but here. Not in his arms.

A chest stands in the corner. I run towards it. His footsteps echo in the distance through the corridor, sounding like they're getting closer. I need to hurry. My fingers shake as they try to open the lid that locks the chest shut. It doesn't budge. A metal lock secures it.

Panicked, I look around. The footsteps grow louder.

"I don't want to hurt you. I just want to talk to you."

The blood drips faster - because my heart is about to leap out of my chest. There's only one option. The table. A white cloth covers it, so large that the fabric almost reaches the floor. Maybe he won't suspect me under it.

With my last strength, I run towards the door that leads from this room to the next and fling it open, making it look like my escape has taken me deeper into the heart of the castle instead of ending here.

He will be here any moment. I can feel him.

Breathless, I drop to my knees and slide under the table.

This moment is the thread from which nightmares are woven.

Everything about the Marquis paralyzes me. His intimidating presence, his self-assurance, and how effortlessly he spoke all the lies over the past months. Everything was so beautiful until he decided to kill me.

"Louise." His voice now fills the hallway outside the room where I hide.

I crouch on the cold floor, clutching my trembling legs. I dare not breathe, but force myself to do so, not wanting to hold my breath and then suddenly gasp for air.

"Darling, where are you?" His tone sounds so gentle, as if he means it.

Desperation stretches through my heart, almost causing it to burst. A whistle cuts through the air, delicate and treacherous. He whistles for me, like calling a dog. "Come out of your hiding place. Don't be so shy."

His leather shoes appear in my field of vision. He stands in the doorway. I wonder if he can smell my fear. My sweat, my disappointment. My tears mixing with blood on my cheeks, forming sad crusts.

Slowly, he enters the room. His calm movements unsettle me. He's too sure to find me here.

"You don't have to be afraid of me."

I swallow.

There's a rushing sound in my ears.

I loved everything about him.

"If you stop running away, it will be over faster and hurt less." Again, he whistles. The tone turns into a melody, melancholic and ancient. It reminds me of the lullabies Mother used to sing to me as a child to lull me to sleep.

He whistles a song.

This is just a game for him.

He has ended so many lives that one more or less makes no difference.

"It wasn't all a lie, Louise. If you come out, I will explain everything to you and you will see that it's different than what you think now."

Blood sticks to his shoes. The blood of my sister.

She betrayed me.

But she was my sister.

A weak moment where she saw no other way out than to sell me doesn't change the fact that half of my heart belongs to her, that we held hands when we were children and scared, and she knows every little and big secret of mine. Knew…

The Marquis crosses the room.

The blood is flowing faster from my nose. When I

try to wipe it from my face, I realize that my fingers are numb. I bite my index finger, but I feel nothing. Something is wrong with me, but I can't find the missing piece of the puzzle. I don't understand what's happening to me.

He stops in the middle of the room, seems to look around. "It's over, Louise. You can't escape from me."

He turns abruptly and his shoe tips now point in my direction. I feel hot and cold at the same time.

"You let me into your soul - and now I will find you everywhere."

It only takes six steps and a confident hand movement for him to snatch the cloth from the table, sealing my fate.

My eyes fill with tears. Desperately, I cling to the gun in my trembling hand.

He kneels before me. He's so tall that he still has to stoop to even see under the tabletop.

I hide my face behind my hands. I don't want this moment to be real. I want to wake up and find myself back in the past.

His scent clouds my senses. He smells like flowers that bloom only at night, like the cold light of the moon.

When his fingers touch mine, I flinch back. He is ice-cold. "There's no point in running anymore," he whispers. "You have to trust me."

He's dead to me, but his beauty is alive and the sound of his velvet voice hypnotizes me. I can't help but look at him.

I expect to see the eyes of a stranger. Instead, there's so much tenderness in his gaze that I almost want to believe that everything is just part of his game, that he will tell me he's tricking Gino and secretly saving me.

But his words kill all hope. "You knew this would happen. Did you really think you were safe by my side?"

He tries to stroke my cheek. I hit his hand, but I grow weaker by the second and he doesn't flinch.

His mouth moves closer to mine. His breath tickles my face. "Don't cry."

For every tear he wipes from my cheek, ten new ones plunge from my eyes into death.

"It will all be over soon."

Something twitches in my chest. I can't suppress the coughing. A gasp escapes from my throat.

I'm in shock and cover my mouth with both hands.

"How much longer do you give her?" Gino's voice is a nightmare come true. I didn't hear him approaching because I was too engrossed in the dark magic of the Marquis, but now that he's here, everything about the old man is too loud. His greedy breathing, his clumsy steps, his malicious laughter.

The Marquis doesn't take his eyes off me as he speaks. "Three minutes. Maybe five."

Acid rises in my mouth.

"I'm proud of you, son. I didn't think you'd do it yourself."

"Only a suicidal man like you would dare to underestimate me," growls the Marquis.

Gino steps up behind him. I only see his sturdy legs and sausage-like fingers as he pats the Marquis on the shoulder in a friendly manner. His Adam's apple twitches. "Women are replaceable."

"Not this one," the Marquis replies with a coldness as if he were Death himself.

"Do you regret your decision?"

"No."

Suddenly I know it. I feel it. That I am dying. My upper body sags forward. With all my strength, I manage to prop myself up on my elbows.

They didn't manage to wound me though... I would have noticed if they had shot me...

Poison!

My throat tightens. This can't be happening. I haven't even had breakfast today.

I search the Marquis' face for clues, but he keeps his lips tightly sealed and his eyes are filled with nothing but pain.

In his gaze, I read everything. How his heart is breaking to lose me - but that he cannot escape his role.

"You miserable bastard," I wheeze. More blood gathers in my mouth than I can swallow. "The champagne." He shows no reaction. "You poisoned me. That's why you wanted to toast with me. You killed me."

He still doesn't say a word.

Not a single fucking word.

Black edges begin to form around my vision. My eyelids grow heavy. At least I can say that I fought. At least I will be reunited with my family.

My head sinks to the ground.

"I still have one question left," I whisper so softly that Gino cannot possibly hear it.

The Marquis brushes a strand of hair from my face. "Whatever you want to know."

I have to close my eyes. If I keep them open, I will lose the strength to speak. So I whisper into the darkness, "Why did you do this?"

His voice in my ear settles over me like a blanket, taking away the pain and filling me with images of what could have been in another life, a more beautiful world.

"Because I love you."

I die.

FORTY-SEVEN
The Marquis

I've seen many dead bodies in my life, but hers is the first that makes me doubt the justice of life.

Her usually pale complexion is now as white as the snow that lay on her father's grave just a few months ago, when I held her hand, supported her arm, and made her believe she could trust me.

Everything I touch dies.

Some say there lies a curse on the Colbert family, that my ancestors traded power for bliss and that each of us is doomed to love unhappily. My heart will never stop beating for her.

Gino sighs contentedly. "It's done."

And I have never wished so much to slit someone's throat as I do in this moment. But I can't. My hands are tied.

I'm a powerful man, but my power is based on my position as chairman of the Circle. I will only hold this position for as long as I'm perceived as strong from the outside.

Gino has doubted my strength. In front of every member of the Circle. If I had given in to my feelings, the cry of my heart, if I had chosen Louise instead of demonstrating that nothing means more to me than power, they would have eliminated me.

Gino lured me into a trap. He knew that I had to

follow the old rules. That he had the right to execute Albert and his family after being betrayed by them. That I had nothing against him.

Gino played the game that my ancestors invented - and it cost me the most precious thing I was ever allowed to possess.

I take her head in both hands. Her expression seems almost peaceful. As if she were sleeping and could wake up at any moment, look at me with her kind eyes, and tell me that I have the choice to be good.

In fairy tales, you just have to want things badly enough to get them. In real life, you get what you fear most. Loneliness.

My index finger traces her eyebrows. She's still warm.

"Remember your promise." Madison's voice sends a cold shiver down my spine - not because I'm afraid of her, but because she embodies everything I despise: spinelessness, opportunism, a love for intrigue.

And yet all of that applies to you as well.

She approaches me. She was once the most beautiful woman on earth to me, now I feel sick just looking at her.

"You promised me that I could spit on her dead body," she says, her red fingernails digging excitedly into her thighs.

I lose control. Faster than I can think, I rise up. My voice is a devastating storm as I shout, "Get out!

Right now! And if you ever dare to mention her name in front of me again, you will find that there are more terrifying fates than dying."

She's pale as chalk.

My hands tremble.

I never lose control.

I'm always composed.

When she still says nothing, just stares at me with an open mouth and slowly shakes her head, I grab her shoulders and firmly push her towards the door.

Gino laughs. "Look at that. So the little one *did* mean more to you than you pretended."

Madison is smart enough to flee down the hallway. Gino, on the other hand, feels too comfortable in his own skin, so he doesn't see my fist in time to dodge it.

Cursing, he slams against the wall, sinks to the ground and holds his bleeding nose with one hand. "You will pay for this."

I go to my knees and grab his neck so tightly that he can barely breathe. "Oh no, my friend, because I *have* already paid. I paid with the one person who ever meant anything to me, and the price was so high that you will be in my debt forever."

Gino tries to wriggle out of my grip, but he's a desperate worm and I'm the embodiment of wrath.

"I loved her. And I killed her. For you. So swallow your dirty words, leave my house, and never show your face near me again."

Gino bares his blood-red teeth. "You forget that I'm

a member of the Circle. You won't get rid of me that easily."

"Trust me. I will find a way."

It takes no further warning to convince him to leave. He huffs loudly as he pulls himself up against the wall and slowly starts moving. A final look, full of contempt, grazes me, then he's gone too.

I'm alone.

Alone with her.

Forever.

Because I distrust Gino, I don't move for several minutes. I breathe as shallowly as possible to detect any possible movement, but he has truly left.

A car door slams in the courtyard. An engine starts.

I go to Louise. She lies on her side, just as she slept in my ancestors' pavilion while I couldn't close my eyes because her beauty filled every corner of my being, and I didn't dare waste a second that I could spend looking at her.

I always suspected that our time was limited. For a brief moment, I didn't want to believe it, but everything we could have had would have always been just an illusion.

All the powerful men in this world want my position.

If they find out that I love, they will know my weak point.

If they find out that I love, they will kill her to bring me down.

That's why the world must believe Louise is dead.

I place a hand on her chest. Her heart is still beating. Weakly, but it's beating. Gently, I stroke her sweat-covered forehead. I can't bear to leave her lying here.

Her body fits perfectly in my arms, and as I carry her into my bedroom, lay her on the soft mattress, and pull the cool silk sheets over her, I could swear she is smiling.

FORTY-EIGHT
The Marquis

Roman leans on the railing of the stairs to the main entrance, as if my castle belonged to him.

Sometimes I envy his audacity, his tendency to risk too much, because perhaps one day he will find his happy ending, while I've closed my book before the story could be told.

His golden hair shines in the sun. He lets his cool gaze wander over the gardens, tapping his toe and unaware of how self-absorbed he looks. How arrogant and proud - and lovable. He will always be my little brother.

"Roman." At the sound of his name, he turns his head. His profile is almost identical to mine. He's the younger version of me.

Curiously, he scans me, searching for wounds, but he will find nothing because I'm only internally injured, where it hurts the most.

Cold spring air burns in my lungs - or is it the thought of Louise?

Roman puts two arms behind him on the railing and leans back relaxed. "Did it go as planned?"

"Yes."

"Then why do you look as if your father had risen from the dead?" When I don't answer, he raises his brows. "Shouldn't you be relieved?"

A NOBLE CONTRACT

The gardeners have planted new lemon trees. The water of the fountains sparkles more precious than any diamond ever could. This paradise is my home, and I should consider myself lucky.

But I feel rejected. Like a stranger who looks at the beauty of life that could have been his own if he weren't so damn egocentric.

"Am I selfish?", I choke out and Roman turns to me in surprise. We don't usually talk about feelings. Our fathers have trained us not to do so.

"Don't take it the wrong way, but that's like asking me if the year has 52 weeks. What do you expect? Of course, you're selfish. You're the most selfish bastard I've ever met," he adjusts his tie. "We have no choice but to think of ourselves. It's the only way to survive."

When I still don't answer, he lets his gaze rest on my face, penetrates my burning soul, and sees through me. "Do you regret killing her?"

My throat tightens.

Hearing it spoken makes it final - that I've lost her.

Roman picks at a piece of skin on his nail bed. "You had no other choice. If you hadn't done it, Gino would have not only destroyed her but you as well."

The trees dance in the wind. What we believe will make us happy is never where we are. The fulfillment of all desires is always hidden in the future, but when I held Louise in my arms, it felt as if nothing else needed to be fulfilled because everything beautiful had already come true.

"She's not dead."

Roman chokes on his spit. "What?"

"I didn't kill her."

His bright eyes burn through my skin. "Tell me that's not true."

I sigh and run my hand through my hair. It hangs in wild strands on my face. I have no strength left to care about my appearance.

I can't bring myself to look at him as I say, "I made her drink a fake poison. So it looked like she were dying."

"By the gods…"

"It has a similar effect to cardiotoxins. The heart slows down, the body feels numb, tired, heavy…"

At the thought of Louise, pushing herself up from the ground with all her strength, fear in her eyes, everything inside me tightens. "And eventually, you lose consciousness. The pulse becomes so weak that you can hardly feel it. My father once sold the powder to a politician who had to flee and fake his death. I found some remnants of it in his old study - that's where I got the idea."

Roman's long fingers trace invisible shapes on the stone railing. "Why?"

"Because I didn't see any other way to save her life."

I can imagine how little sense I make to him. I myself feel nothing but confusion and helplessness.

So I let the words flow without thinking too much about them. "I knew that Gino wouldn't stop hunting

Louise until she was dead. And my hands were tied. Her father made a mistake. It was Gino's right to avenge that mistake. There was no loophole, no way to convince the Circle to let her live. If I had stood up for her just because she's my wife, then people would have started to believe that different rules apply to me, that I'm using my position for personal gain."

Roman nods but remains silent. I have his full attention.

"I would never have let her die. Dogs like Gino deserve to rot, but not innocents. Louise had nothing to do with the whole thing. She deserved to live. When Gino told me that Charlotte had approached him to make a deal, I realized that Louise was not safe anywhere in the world, not even with her own family - that she had to go into hiding, disappear and start a new life somewhere no one knows her. Damn it, her sister even invented a kiss that never happened just to manipulate Louise and distance her from me."

The midday sun breaks through the gray clouds. Warm light falls on my face, but everything inside me is cold.

I didn't love her from the first moment, but when I started loving her, I knew it was forever.

"I knew she would never give up without a fight. That she would never agree to run away from Gino. That's why I pretended to agree with his plan and lured them both into a trap. He now thinks he has eliminated her while she gets to live on."

"Without you." Roman's words cut right through

my heart because he's right.

"Without me. She will never forgive me for lying to her."

"And for killing her sister."

"She betrayed Louise."

"That still won't undo it. She will never be able to forget that her sister is dead because of you. Believe me..." - he pats me on the shoulder - "if anyone were to harm you, I would chase them to the ends of the earth."

I believe him wholeheartedly. "If I hadn't made sacrifices, Gino would have seen through my charade. He had to believe that I was serious, that it wasn't about protecting Louise. Killing Charlotte was the only credible proof in his eyes that I stood on his side."

Roman tilts his head back. "Holy shit. You've really gotten yourself into something." He laughs. "You saved the woman you love and lost her forever at the same time."

I would trade all my possessions, the old cars, the rare horses, the enchanted castles, for a single minute where I can hold her in my arms one last time. "I will fight for her."

"Good luck with that. She managed to crack your tough shell, so she'll be strong enough to resist your charm as well. Everything you tell her from now on will sound like lies in her ears, even if it's the truth - and in every move you make, she'll see the one who brought down her sister."

I can hear the horses neighing as the stable boy leads them out to pasture. The midday air tastes like summer.

"What should I do?"

The question hangs between us like an unsolved puzzle. Roman furrows his brow in surprise. I've never asked him for advice; usually, he comes to me when he needs help.

"The only thing you can do is try to talk to her. Explain everything to her. I don't believe she will forgive you, but if you don't try, you'll regret it forever."

Try. I've never had to try anything in my life because I was always sure in advance that I would win. I've never doubted my strength - until Louise came along. Because she opened my eyes and made me understand that true strength does not stem from punches and extortion, but from the courage to make oneself vulnerable by believing in love.

"She won't want to listen to me."

"If that's the case, you have no choice but to let her go. But at least try. You have nothing to lose."

A NOBLE CONTRACT

FORTY-NINE

Most people fear their end. They push the thought of their own mortality aside for a lifetime, and when the moment comes for death to bestow its merciless kiss upon them, they are not prepared to die.

I have never feared death. Not my own. I have always been afraid of losing those who reside in my heart, but leaving myself behind has never been a dark thought for me.

Perhaps because I always assumed that I would fill my life with adventures, with midnight kisses from strangers, travels to forgotten places, and countless books read by the sea.

I have never felt afraid of death because secretly, I wanted to believe that I had time. Time to make all my dreams come true. It was an illusion.

Death feels less powerful than I imagined it. Less final. I see nothing. I feel nothing. But the memories are there.

I have always assumed that everything dissolves into thin air when the time comes to go, that one is carried away into an insatiable nothingness, but instead everything is still within me: my sister's laughter, the dog we got for Christmas as children, Gabriel's friendship, and the brief love of the

Marquis.
I feel my life in my chest.
And I breathe...

When I open my eyes, everything feels strange. My own body is so heavy that it pulls me down like an anchor. I can't move my legs.

My head is pounding. Memories are slowly coming back. Blood. Tears. Betrayal.

I look around.

Despite my mistakes, I've always hoped to go to heaven. When I recognize the Marquis' bedroom, I come to the bitter realization that I have landed in hell.

Is this a devil's joke? That I will be forever trapped in the castle where I lost my heart and never found it again?

I hear footsteps in the hallway. Isn't it said that the first person you meet in the afterlife is the soul you will be eternally connected to?

The doorknob turns. Spellbound, I stare at the opening door - expecting Charlotte or my parents... but am bitterly disappointed.

Him. Of all the people I have shared my life with, it has to be the man I feel nothing but pure hatred for who appears before me first?

He looks identical to how he did just before my death. The same black suit, the same tousled dark blond hair.

Only his expression is different. Alien. Full of

remorse and broken heart.

The door falls shut behind him. He leans against it with his back. All exits are blocked. "You're awake," he says softly.

I can't say a word.

"I didn't expect you to be awake already."

Hell feels dangerously similar to real life. Maybe that's what makes it such a terrible place.

The Marquis takes a step towards me. Instinctively, I recoil, but I'm too weak to get up from the bed.

"Don't be afraid."

Anger rises within me and I finally find my voice again. "I'm not afraid. I have nothing left in me. Only hatred."

He flinches almost imperceptibly, but I notice it. "Just give me five minutes - to explain everything."

Slowly, very slowly, a realization swims through the dark ocean of my subconscious and struggles to the surface...

I smell his cologne.

My heart skips a beat.

The realization emerges.

"I'm not dead. I survived."

With wide eyes, I look down at myself. Dark brown stains run across my dress. Dried blood. I am alive.

"Oh God," I exclaim. "Oh God, oh God, oh God." I need to get out of here before he will kill me *again*. I have to escape from him. But there's only one door and he's blocking the way. He's an angel of death.

I gasp for air. "What have I done to you? Why do you hate me so much that you want to kill me not just once but twice?" My lower lip trembles.

He takes a deep breath. "I don't want to kill you. You would understand that if you just listened to me for a moment."

"I don't want to hear any more of your lies."

"I'm not lying. I promise."

"Your promises are worthless."

Frustrated, he runs both hands through his hair. "What do I have to do for you to believe that I don't want to hurt you?"

"Let me go."

It's not the answer he was hoping for. But he knows he has lost me forever. I see it in his empty eyes.

"Fine. I'll let you go. If you listen to me first."

I press my lips together tightly.

"Five minutes, Louise. No more."

"Okay." It's my only way out of here. He wants to take another step towards me, but I raise my hands defensively. "Don't come any closer."

It's clear that I'm hurting him, and it fills me with satisfaction to see him suffer. This is just the beginning…

"I did it to protect you."

"That sounds a lot like the words of a narcissist. I won't let myself be manipulated by you any longer."

"Gino would have killed you if I hadn't pretended

to beat him to it. I gave you a fake poison so he would think you were dead."

My breath catches. I am surprised and not surprised at the same time.

"I knew he wouldn't rest until you were dead. So I outsmarted him."

I can't speak. There are no words that could do this moment justice. All the anger, disappointment, shock.

"I've prepared everything for you, Louise. You will fly to Argentina on my jet. I have already rented a house for you there. You will get new documents and a new name of your choice."

Because I say nothing, he speaks faster and faster, as if he feels me slipping away from him.

"You will have personal protection at any time. I'll pay for everything. I promise you that nothing can happen to you. I'll take care of you."

My knees are trembling. I feel sick. Because I still love him. I love the fragile undertone in his voice when he takes off the mask of the villain. I love his big hands, with which he could protect me from any harm if he wanted to. I love the green of his eyes, in which it is written that he really loves me, even though he will never be able to show it to me in a healthy way.

"Are you expecting me to be grateful?"

He swallows. "No. I expect nothing from you."

"Then why are you telling me all this?"

"Because I hope that one day you can forget that I'm a monster and find something in yourself that makes it possible for you to forgive me."

"Why didn't you involve me earlier?"

"Because I knew you would never agree with my plan. And because your fear of death had to seem realistic to Gino."

"You made me believe that I was dying..."

"I didn't mean to hurt you with that."

"Hurt?" My voice becomes loud. "Hurt would mean that you speak ill of me behind my back or secretly kiss someone else. You didn't hurt me. You destroyed me."

Tears in his eyes. They mean nothing to me.

"You pretended for months that I could rely on you. I entrusted you with my sister's life, begged you to save her. Instead... instead, you were the one who..." I can't bring myself to say it.

He falls to his knees in front of me. His beautiful face is distorted with despair.

"I'm so sorry, Louise. I hate myself. You can't imagine how much. I knew I would lose you and still did it. Because I couldn't bear the thought of you dying."

He collapses. "I would do it again. I would kill every person in this world if it meant you lived."

I determinedly throw back the covers, moving towards him with weary bones and heavy breath. My hands find his. We lock eyes.

"I loved you, Jerome. And I still love you. Your kisses drowned my pain when I didn't know how to go on."

He breathes a sigh of relief.

"But I will never forgive you for what you did."

He grabs my wrists.

"Louise, please..." The pain in his voice steals a piece of my soul. Leaving him will be my end. But I am already broken. There is only one thing that keeps me breathing. Revenge.

"Listen to me carefully. I will learn how to enter locked rooms unnoticed. I will learn how to secretly stalk someone without being seen. I will learn at what angle to hold a knife to cut a throat in one motion. And I will find you..."

I wrench my hands away from him. He groans.

"I will take everything that matters to you. I won't rest until you beg me on your knees to disappear from your life, and then... I will kill you. Gino, Madison, you. Your brother. I will make you suffer and only be satisfied when your blood has dried on my hands."

I open the door. I have no idea where to go because I know I have no home left in this world and no one who loves me the way I deserve to be loved, but one thing remains: the certainty that I am a good person.

"You know, Marquis," I speak to him one last time without looking at him. "I'm not as influential as you, not as rich or important... no one will notice if I disappear." He flinches. "But at least I never betrayed or sold anyone out. Especially not myself."

He is just a shadow of himself.

A NOBLE CONTRACT

His eyes plead with me not to leave.
I slam the door behind me.

EPILOGUE

My heart is too heavy for my chest - too full of bitter disappointment and piercing pain.

I have always felt too much and over the years I have come to terms with it, but feeling too much for the wrong person is a poison for which humanity has not yet found an antidote.

The certainty that we could have been happy gnaws at my heart, if only he had been honest and less in love with the power that will never be his, because nothing we humans possess accompanies us into death.

Nothing, except love. It is the only thing we leave behind when we go, when people who loved us keep the memory of us alive.

The castle smells of him.

Of nights when the air crackled with electricity, of secret kisses and daydreams of his bare chest against mine.

I hold my breath.

My heart beats too fast.

I feel dizzy.

I have no idea where my luggage is, whether it's still in the mirrored hall where I left it during my escape, or if one of the servants has already started to throw my things away. It doesn't matter anymore.

In the life I begin today, my old name is nothing

but a faint echo, a forgotten melody. I will create a new self. I will disappear and reappear at the exact moment when they least expect me.

I am revenge.

I am darkness.

I am everything the world never expected me to be.

Printed in Great Britain
by Amazon